HIDDEN IN
SEALSKIN

by Thea van Diepen

Behold, the requisite legal material:

Cover design: Roberto Calas
Author photo: Katie Leonardo
Editor: EJ Clark of Silver Jay Media

Published by: Thea van Diepen
Ebook ISBN: 978-0-9916993-8-4
Paperback ISBN: 978-0-9916993-7-7

This is a work of fiction. Any resemblance the
characters, settings, or events have to
real people, places, or events
is completely unintentional.

Otherwise, we'd have some crazy uncanny valley *bleep* going on here.

To my Oma and Opa.
You will never read this but, nonetheless:
This is for you.

For everyone on the Puttytribe:
By your presence,
support,
and encouragement,
you have changed my life.
Thank you.

Pider shoved Adren against the wall, hands at either side of her head, pressed so hard against the stone she could see the muscles in his arms straining. She angled her head so as to see out of the alleyway, but Pider shook his head and grunted. He bent his head low over hers.

Even with that smallest of glimpses, Adren had been able to make out the lamplighter on her way through the evening fog and the trail of lights behind her. Adren opened her mouth to ask why they were hiding from the woman, but Pider pressed her mouth closed. He swallowed, Adam's apple bobbing, then again with another swallow. Adren couldn't make sense of it. There was no need to fear, and yet she could see the tendons in Pider's neck straining against his skin. He breathed in shallow spurts, and his body shook, though that lessened after his second swallow.

Pider raised his eyebrows, looking directly at Adren, and lessened the pressure of his fingers on her lips. She nodded.

He stepped back, angling his head away from the street.

Adren raised an eyebrow.

Pider lowered his, shaking his head more emphatically than before, then he mimed lifting a hood. At first, Adren narrowed her eyes, confused, but then she remembered. Her

5

hair. She put her hood over her head, taking care to tuck any stray locks back where they wouldn't be seen.

Hands in his pockets, Pider adopted a casual stance. As the lamplighter lit the streetlight nearest them, Pider's eyes flicked towards her, his hands lumping into fists beneath the fabric of his pants. His pupils were dilated, more so than Adren had expected even with the darkness of the alley. The lamplighter passed them without a pause in her stride and lit the next lamp. Pider's shoulders slumped, most of the tension gone from them. They both waited, his head tilted in the lamplighter's direction, eyes anxious. Adren watched him. Why was he so scared?

Before long, Pider checked the street and nodded at Adren. They crossed it, entering the alley on the other side. They continued on their way, walking on the wet cobblestone, the roofs of houses still dripping from that evening's rain. The air pressed around them, damp not only with the fog, but also the promise of more rain. Pider's gait had quickened since the crossing, and his back become a little more hunched over. Much as Adren wanted to ask for an explanation, she took nearly two steps for each one of his, and had to work so hard to keep up that she had no breath left to speak.

The alley took a sudden snakelike twist, but Adren kept close to Pider. She had little experience with human communities and so, without his help, would have become lost in only a few moments, especially now that it had become dark. The only problem at this moment was her hood, which narrowed her peripheral vision more than was comfortable, so she lowered it again and let her hair fall ghostlike behind her.

As soon as Adren could make out the light spilling from the next crossing, Pider stopped to open the gate in a high wooden fence. Adren tried to peer through the chinks, but the posts pressed together too tightly and she could not see beyond them. Hinges creaked as Pider opened the gate and beckoned to Adren, his eyes searching the way they had come. She passed through into a small, unkempt yard, the grass like hair in need of a good brushing. Pider walked by her and up to the door. He knocked, four quick beats, then a pause, then two beats. The door opened to reveal a hatchet-faced man. He stood aside to let Pider and Adren enter.

Inside, the house was dimly lit. Adren could make out cracks in the plaster on the walls.

"Shoes," said the man before he scuttled off. Pider removed his and Adren followed suit, placing hers close to the door on one end of a line of shoes, at least ten pairs in total. She frowned.

"Must be something going on tonight," Pider said.

"I suppose," Adren replied. "But so late?"

"Parties go late." He shrugged.

"Look, Pider, we're not doing anything wrong, are we? You acted like you were afraid of the lamplighter seeing us."

"Oh, her. We had a bit of a falling out not too long ago. I've been avoiding her... She's still really angry at me about it all." His eyebrows drew together in a peculiar way, so quickly that Adren wouldn't have seen it if she weren't paying such close attention to his body language, and especially his eyes, which hadn't left hers since she'd asked her question. Pider was lying to her, no doubt about it, but most likely only to avoid having to tell an embarrassing story. She wondered what had really gone on between him and the lamplighter.

He seemed to notice her hesitation.

"I promise the cure's here, though. And it's real. I checked to make sure, after you told me about all the disappointments you've had."

Adren smiled. "You keep telling me. Thank you."

"So, do we go in?" He indicated the rest of the house.

"Yes."

Pider led her through to a dark door, though there was too little light at this point to discern more.

"You go in first," he said. "He'll be expecting you."

Adren took a deep breath. After two years of looking, here it was: A cure for madness. And so much closer to home than she had expected, too. She wanted to remember every detail, right down to the feel of her feet against the rough wooden floor.

Exhaling, she nodded. Pider opened the door, and she went in.

The door slammed shut behind her, plunging the room into utter blackness. Hands grabbed at her. She tried to fight them, but there seemed to be more than one attacker and, before long, they held her fast.

"We got her," a male voice called, and Pider entered through the door—which was now to Adren's right—a lamp in one hand. He placed it on the table near the other end of the room as the hatchet-faced man also entered, pen and paper in hand. Behind him came two more men who stayed by the door. What was going on?

"She's such a little thing," said one of the men who held Adren. "You sure you need all of us to keep her still?"

"I am," said Pider. Adren's heart pounded louder at the coldness in his voice. He adjusted the lamp so that it burned a little brighter. "Keep your eyes on her. Changelings are tricky creatures. She can turn invisible if you look away."

"I told you I don't know what I am," said Adren, straining against the men's hold.

"Yes, well, you still can't deny that 'the White Changeling' has a certain ring to it," commented the hatchet-faced man. Pider wrinkled his nose and glared sideways at the man, who sat down at once and busied himself with straightening his papers.

"I really don't care what you are," Pider said. "Where is the unicorn, Adren?"

"Pider, tell me this is a misunderstanding." She wanted this not to be real but, if it wasn't, then it was far more convincing than any nightmare had a right to be. Not that she would call it a nightmare quite yet. Perhaps Pider had simply heard some untruth about her that caused him to distrust her.

Pider snorted and crossed his arms. He gave a half smile. "You don't expect me to believe that you'd let a mad unicorn just run around where it pleases, do you? Now, where is it?" Beside him, the hatchet-faced man stared at Adren, pen in hand.

"I don't know."

"Liar!" He slapped her, causing tears. "Tell me where it is!"

"Why are you—?"

Pider punched her, and everything went black.

When Adren awoke, she was still in the same room, only now she was tied to a chair with thick rope, her arms stiff at her sides. Pider and the hatchet-faced man were still by the table, and the men who had held her stood around and behind her.

She had been kidnapped. Kidnapped that they might find the unicorn and use it. But hadn't Pider helped her before? Wasn't he supposed to be trustworthy? Adren hadn't thought that humans could do such terrible things. And yet, they were doing them to her, and wanted to do more to the unicorn. Part of her realized this coldly, analytically, but another felt only pain.

And then there was the dark part of her mind, the part she could never see into, and something in it was stirring. Another heartbeat? She kept her thoughts away, afraid to find out what might emerge.

"Now that you've had some time to think," Pider said, picking up a heavy wooden staff, "where is the unicorn?"

"I don't know!"

"You know what we could do with you if you don't tell us?" He came in close, so close that when he whispered to her, she could feel his breath tickle her cheek.

"People... *like* that?" Adren wanted to vomit.

"And for you they'll pay a good deal of money, too." Pider stroked her cheek with one finger, the brown of his skin in stark contrast to the white of hers. "Exotic little thing that you are."

Desperate, Adren tried to bite him, but he snapped back his hand too quickly. She felt claustrophobic with so many people in the room. It wasn't a large room and, with all those men surrounding her... the hairs on the back of her neck rose, and sensation heightened. Each flicker of the lamp, no matter how slight, caught her attention as well as when it had just been lit.

"Where is the unicorn?"

"I don't know." There was steel in her words, but its strength wavered. It didn't matter what he threatened, she couldn't tell him anything other than the truth, and she would suffer for it.

The dark part of her mind shifted, as whatever stirred inside separated and began to establish itself. It coiled tight against the back of her skull, almost like the rope around her body, but then it loosened and stretched outwards to some unknown location, reaching and reaching until, finally, it opened.

"I'm done being patient with you," Pider said. He hefted the staff, then slammed it into Adren's side. Pain filled her, pain and the fear of what else, what worse could happen. Part of it slipped out through that opening in her mind.

"Tell me where the unicorn is!" he yelled.

"I *can't!*" said Adren, her voice cracking on the second word. Through the opening came alarm, then understanding, then determination, all threaded through with a wild beat, leaning towards chaos. Something was coming. Not inside, not through that connection in her mind. Whatever it was Adren was connected to, it was coming. Coming for her.

She couldn't hear what was being said around her, only that there were voices. It was too painful to listen, and too overwhelming to hear. Her emotions and the emotions of this other thing flowed back and forth, a conversation she could barely comprehend, one that her mind felt too small to contain. Barely, she felt the ropes around her fall away, then hands on her arms as she was dragged off. She started shaking, and the determination of the other thing came through even stronger, as did the feeling that it was coming closer and closer.

"Help me," Adren whispered. "Help me."

Someone picked her up. She caught a glimpse of the roof, of the sky. There was the creak of the gate. The feel of wood as her head brushed the fence. The sound of shoes against cobblestone.

A piercing scream.

A creature like a deer, but white and with a single horn spiralling out from its forehead. The unicorn charged, wild, and most of the men scattered. A few stood their ground, only to cry out and fall from the flash of hooves and the plunge of the horn. The man holding Adren dropped her. She only had a moment or two to prepare before crashing into the ground, enough for energy to surge through her. Praying to all the saints that none of the men were paying attention, Adren made herself invisible and crawled to the fence. Half-crouched, she pressed herself against it and rocked a little on her heels. She had to get control of herself before she couldn't hold the invisibility any longer.

Anger and pain flowed through the connection, throb for throb with what Adren could piece together of the unicorn in battle before her. The unicorn. Her dear, mad unicorn. Just this knowledge, small though it was, tamed the chaos around her. It didn't matter—much as she wanted to know—how long this connection had existed, whether it had been created that day or merely been obscured by the dark, or what the exact nature of this connection was. What mattered was that whatever Adren felt, the unicorn received through the connection. And, based on what had just happened, the unicorn returned it with even greater intensity. If she couldn't calm her emotions and make sense of her surroundings again… she didn't want to experience what would happen next.

Adren closed her eyes. Breathed. The unicorn's rage, its pain, gripped her, clawing at her heart and skin.

But it was not hers.

She had to convince herself of that. She had to experience it as truth. The unicorn's emotions were those of a foreigner in her country, and could not affect her. They remained separate from her own emotions, separate and disconnected.

It helped, allowing Adren to calm to the point where, if she wanted, she could open her eyes without being overwhelmed. Her senses cleared, returning to something like order, and the tension in her chest, the result of holding onto invisibility for so long, rose to prominence. It would turn to pain soon, and then her grip would start to falter if she did not let go and rest from the exertion. But was she safe? She opened her eyes.

Most of the men had fled, and the few who hadn't lay in the alleyway. Blood stained the cobblestones, and had spattered on the forelegs and flanks of the unicorn, who stood, breathing heavily, eyes in a frantic search of the surroundings. As soon as

Adren let herself become visible again, the unicorn walked over to her and lowered its head so that its forehead was nearly level with hers. She pressed her face against its and stroked it oh-so-gently under its jaw.

"Thou," she said, slipping into the dialect she was most used to. "I am glad thou'rt here."

The unicorn's tension rang through their new connection, sharp and discordant. It was difficult not to return that or worse, but Adren held fast and let herself feel only tenderness. In response, the unicorn relaxed, which Adren could both feel through the connection and see as the unicorn's taut muscles became soft again. Its eyes closed.

Adren rose to her feet, wincing at the complaints of her legs, uncomfortable from crouching so long. The fence-gate creaked but, when she looked, she could find no one else up and conscious, so she stretched, lulled by the unicorn's gentle thrum of contentment in the back of her mind. This connection fascinated her. How did it work? What were its limits?

She opened her eyes only to see Pider, knife in hand, about to stab the unicorn. Energy rushed through Adren. As the unicorn shied away, its fear spiking into her mind, she grabbed Pider's arm. He strained against her, but she forced his arm down, leaving his body open. With a quick in-out, she punched him in the gut. He doubled over, and she twisted, back to him, to wrestle the knife out of his hand. As soon as she had it, his other arm snaked over her body.

Well, she had a knife. She shifted her hold and stabbed him in the side. Pider cried out, and Adren slipped out of his grasp, leaving the knife in him. Teeth clenched, he reached for the hilt sticking out of his side.

"Don't!" said Adren. Pider paused. Too quickly for him to react, she pulled out the knife herself. She twisted the blade in his flesh as she did, making the wound larger. "It was keeping you from bleeding." Sure enough, a red stain spread out on his shirt following the knife's removal.

They stared at each other a moment, Adren with her knife

ready. Pider's hand hovered over his wound as his eyes flicked up and down this young woman whose head only came to his shoulders. Those shoulders rounded, and he pressed his hand into his side with a grimace, body already turned for flight.

"Listen to me carefully, Pider." Now the steel in her words didn't waver. "If you ever try to harm me or the unicorn again, I will kill you myself."

He ran.

Adren waited until a little after she could no longer see him before she turned to the unicorn and put a hand on its flank. A refrain, its rhythm keeping time with her footsteps, pounded through her head all the way home.

Never again.

Now

Chapter One

They had found her.

Footsteps thudded against the packed dirt of the streets behind Adren as she ran. She made a nimble turn onto the next and wove through and around the pedestrians, the carts, the animals. Behind her, the security officers yelled and fumbled past the obstacles. They knew the town far better than she, but that only gave them a slight advantage: Adren's stamina and agility more than made up for her lack of navigational skills.

Adren spied an alley ahead. A quick glance behind told her that she still didn't have enough lead to lose the officers simply by making the turn. It would have to serve only to slow them for now. She ducked in, senses alert to any twists she could use to her advantage and any dead ends she could not.

The buildings loomed close in the alley. They amplified the voices of the officers and, it seemed, Adren's own breathing. Her flesh crawled at the narrowness of the space. She glanced back again. The officers were still a decent way behind her, but there appeared to be fewer of them. Adren did a quick count. Yes. Definitely fewer. They must have split up at the alley entrance. Everything drew in closer around Adren, the light harsher, the sounds more discordant, the smell...

No. Now was not the time to panic. They thought they could

cut her off, did they? Well, then.

The alley took a sharp turn and then forked. To the left, it continued to wend its way behind and between. To the right, it opened out onto a quiet street. Adren couldn't see any officers on it yet, but she was certain it was only a matter of time. She made herself invisible and turned right.

The missing officers shot out from the street and barrelled down the alley. They shouted at their comrades behind Adren, asking them where she was. The officers behind her, who would have only seen her form waver, replied that she was right there, and to grab her before she got to the street, you idiots. This offended the officers in front, who stopped, shot off a barrage of insults at their fellows, and berated them for losing her.

Adren grinned. She darted past the stalled officers and onto the street, letting go of her invisibility as she did. Commotion ensued in the alley, and she would have laughed if she didn't think it would to draw more attention to herself. Instead, she let her mirth pass through the back of her mind and to the unicorn, who responded in kind.

It wouldn't take long before they reorganized themselves, so Adren scanned the street for somewhere to hide. It was nearly empty, mostly made up of houses in need of repair and a few boarded-up shops. The few people there didn't even look up as Adren ran past. Perfect.

The chaos behind her had become purposeful again. She could tell just from listening that she had increased her lead, but not by much. It was time to find a hiding place.

None of the buildings presented a simple solution. The problem with residential areas was that people kept their doors closed and, in an area like this, locked as well. A few had fenced yards, and Adren entertained the idea of leaping over them for a moment before shaking her head. She didn't have the height for that. What she needed was an empty building, an abandoned shop that wasn't quite boarded up enough, a barn.

A barn?

Yes, there was an old livery barn on the corner. If she could get into a stall quickly enough, she should be able to turn invisible without anyone seeing her and negating the magic. Well. Without any humans seeing her. It could work. She made the turn and, spotting the entrance, crashed through the doors.

But there were no stalls. The barn didn't even have any inner walls. All it had were support beams and a ladder at one end leading up to a trap door. She could hear the officers nearing the corner. Gods in hell.

It would have to do.

She raced to the ladder and clambered up. Her body out of sight, she held onto the top of the ladder with all her might and made it invisible.

Before long, the officers came to the barn entrance. Their voices echoed through the barn as they decided what to do now that they'd lost sight of Adren. A few were sent to search the street, a few to wait and see if she'd double back, and two entered the barn. Their boots squeaked on the floorboards as they walked the length and breadth of the dingy space.

One stopped under the trapdoor, and Adren had to keep herself from peeking through the opening in case he looked up and saw her. She held her breath, which did nothing to help the slow-growing tightness in her chest, and hoped the officer didn't bump into the ladder and make it fall from her grasp.

The officers outside called into the barn, and the one under the trapdoor replied that the barn was empty. He and the other left, and Adren started breathing again. She was about to release the invisibility, too, when she heard the officers, still in front of the barn and in clear view of where the ladder would reappear, conferring amongst themselves. Her hand ached. Her chest ached. The officers continued to pool details to come up with a consistent and disconcertingly accurate description of her. She'd have to find a dye shop before the morning was out. Hadn't she seen one earlier? If only she could remember where.

Would those officers ever leave? Adren's heart felt like it barely had space to beat, and she had to keep her breaths shallow to avoid pain.

Another voice joined those of the officers, the polite voice of a boy or young man. The officers grew quiet, and one explained the situation to the newcomer, asking him if he had seen Adren. The boy said he hadn't, and then asked them to leave, saying they were disturbing his ill mother's sleep. With apologies, the officers left. Then the barn doors closed.

Adren waited, ears straining, but she didn't hear anyone inside the barn. She let go of the ladder. Her body sagged in relief as the tension of keeping up the magic drained away.

"Well," said the boy's voice from inside the barn. "That's interesting." Footsteps came next, and then the ladder shook.

Adren's muscles tightened and she made herself invisible out of reflex. Everything within her protested; it was too soon, but there was no helping it. Magic held in place, she watched as a face peeked up through the opening. The boy was older than she had thought, too young to be considered a man, but only barely clinging to childhood. He looked right at Adren. She tried to convince herself that she had become invisible in time but, as he got up, his eyes never left her.

"And now it makes sense."

Adren pushed the boy into the wall as hard as she could, and then she flew down the ladder and out of the barn. That cure had better be worth all the trouble. Robbing Lord Watorej's private vault hadn't been her best idea, but with the potion maker's prices, Adren hadn't had many other options. Certainly not any that would have worked this quickly.

It wasn't until she had neared the dye shop that she remembered to check her coat pocket for the money. Yes, it was all there. Twenty thousand keb. Or five hundred olen, however you wanted to count. Plus some extra, for emergencies. None had fallen out during the chase. As she stood before the entrance, Adren congratulated herself on her foresight. Hair and skin as light as hers never went unnoticed, no matter how big the town, and the potion maker's shop was clear on the other end of this one. Now that the officers had seen her, she had to blend in, and that cost money.

Still, she hesitated. Visible through the shop windows was a crowd of both humans and vivid fabrics and dyes. It would be difficult to escape once entered, if the need arose. A customer exited, and the door's swing set off chimes with a ringing that hurt Adren's ears. What was it about humans and noise?

Adren took a breath, then opened the door to step inside. A conflicted collection of odours enveloped her, emanating from a section of perfumes and scented candles. The bright oranges, reds, yellows, and blues of clothing and rolls of fabric attacked her eyes, their brightness a sword. A burst of laughter came from one corner as the shopkeep, bangles jangling, regaled customers with the values of silk, her hands jabbing the air with every syllable. Two women pressed by, arms full of goods, while they whispered and shot furtive glances at Adren. A clock ticked in the back, each pulse a stab of pain in her skull, each pulse a cue for the walls to inch in ever closer. It took her a bit to steady herself before she could enter, in time for the door to swing shut and set off the chimes again. She shuddered and tried to make her way to the dyes without being noticed.

"What can I help you with, my dear?" No such luck. Adren turned to face the shopkeep, whose voice was so strident and expression so delighted that Adren considered strangling her.

"This." Adren picked up a small roll of sturdy white fabric. She really did intend on buying it—she had run short of bandages. Its more immediate function, however, was to keep from being subjected to a sales pitch. The shopkeep, obviously disappointed in such a plain choice, focused her attention on Adren's appearance, as if to find a way to remedy such frugal taste. She wrinkled her nose at the worn clothing, but her lips curved slightly when she appraised Adren's face.

"Such a pretty girl like you would surely want something more colourful. A bold red would contrast splendidly, or a blue to bring out your eyes? This," she dismissed the fabric in Adren's hand, bangles clanking, "this would wash you out, make you sickly. You don't want it; it would be a poor purchase."

"I do, in fact, want it. It and two bottles of dye. Brown and black." Adren indicated them with a jab of her chin.

"Oh, no, that is too simple, too demure. Come with me—" at this point, the shopkeep tried to put an arm around Adren, surely expecting unmeant protests and submission, as any girl of her age in that town would react to an elder. Adren stepped away, neatly avoiding the arm.

"Stop trying to squeeze money out of me, or I'll leave without purchasing." She kept her words quiet enough to avoid attracting notice, low and threaded with steel. The shopkeep frowned when she saw Adren's hand move, as if by reflex, to her hip. Her eyes flicked up to Adren's face, but Adren gave no indication that the threat had been made on purpose.

The shopkeep pursed her lips and retrieved the bottles of dye. She then went to the counter and made a great display of looking up prices.

"Thirty keb."

"Does this look like perfume and silk to you? Four and one." A small child started wailing from somewhere in the middle of the shop. The air seemed to thicken in response, and it took all Adren had to keep her breath even. She took out the money from her pocket. The shopkeep grabbed it and handed over the dye, her expression sour.

"I'll serve you today," she said, "but do not return. You darken the room with your manner."

"Good. It needs the darkness."

After dyeing her hair and skin in a public bathroom, Adren went to the potion maker's shop. This took longer than she had expected—the sun was setting by the time she arrived—and she longed to be out of the town. This was, of course, the most appropriate moment to discover that the door was locked. Adren swore. Then, containing her frustration, she knocked more or less politely.

"If she doesn't come to the door then, saints help me…"

The curtain on the window drew back and the potion maker peeked through. She proceeded to fail to recognize Adren and pointed at a sign on the door that Adren couldn't read.

Adren responded by pulling out some some of the money. On the surface, this seemed to confuse the potion maker, but her eyes gleamed with interest. She opened the door.

"The store's closed. Can't you read the sign?"

"You mentioned that," Adren said drily. "I have the price you quoted for a madness cure." The woman peered at Adren.

"That was you?"

"Would I have said that otherwise? Let me in, and never mind how I look now."

"Show me," said the potion maker as she pulled the door slightly closed. Adren sighed.

"I'm not showing you all the money while I'm standing out on the street where everyone can see. Unless you want thieves coming by later tonight to claim your earnings."

The potion maker made a sound of displeasure, but she let Adren inside, locking the door and closing the curtains after.

"Now, show me."

Adren obliged and pulled out the bills one by one, counting as she went, using the pictures to identify their value, watching how the potion maker's eyes widened with each increase.

"Twenty thousand keb, which makes five hundred olen, exactly as you asked. Your turn." She kept in her pocket the extra fifty and forty-five that she had stolen for herself.

"How did you get all of this so quickly?" asked the potion maker as she snatched up the bills.

Adren raised an eyebrow.

"Well, then..." The woman cleared her throat. "It's just that... I... well. I didn't expect anyone to be able to come up with that much money." She paused.

"And?"

"I... er, that is to say, I was trying to make you go away. To be completely honest, I cannot make you the cure." Gods. This woman could not possibly be serious.

"Explain." Adren's was not a hot anger, the kind that would explode and slop around. Rather, it froze, bringing a calm to her body like that in the eye of a storm. Her voice remained utterly

23

level, but the same steel she had partially unveiled earlier that day for the shopkeep now lay naked in her tone.

"It's not that I don't have the knowledge or the skill," said the potion maker, her words coming out in a rush, "It's only that I don't have the tools. One tool in particular." She stared at the money. "The lord has it. He stole it from me years ago in punishment for an imagined slight. If I had it, I would be able to make the cure, and a great deal more besides."

For obvious reasons, Adren did not want to break into the lord's mansion. Also, depending on what the tool happened to be, searching for and transporting it could be difficult.

"What is this tool?"

"It's a jewel. You wouldn't be able to get it, would you?"

"That depends."

"Well, it houses magic I need for the most potent potions I am able to make, but you won't find it by looking for it. What you need to find is its case, which is a sealskin. Only I know how to get the jewel out of it, so you won't be able to check, but you'll know when you find it."

Adren could see the possibility in this scenario. Unfortunately, using a sealskin as a jewel case was one of the more ridiculous things that Adren had heard over the past few years. She paused and took a breath. Reminded herself how far she'd already come, and how far she intended to go.

"How will I know it when I see it?" Adren crossed her arms.

"Who would keep an old sealskin around if not for what it contained?" The potion maker shrugged. "You'll know."

"Where is it?"

At this, the potion maker's expression fell. "I don't know. It's most likely locked up somewhere in the mansion, not the vault, seeing as his steward and accountants would have access to that, but somewhere only he has access to, because of its magic. Which could be anywhere."

"How remarkably helpful." This whole situation set her teeth on edge, but what other options did she have? There had been so many failures…

24

The unicorn's terror spiked, the emotion followed close by pain. Due to its insanity, it had a tendency to find danger, and if it got free, it would come running to her. If it didn't... well. Either way, Adren couldn't stay any longer. If she needed more information, she would have to return in the morning.

"You'll be able to get it?"

"We will just have to see, won't we?" Adren turned and headed to the door.

"Don't you want to negotiate the payment?"

"I don't care about payment. All I want is the cure, yesterday." She let the door swing shut as she headed down the street, pulling her coat tighter against the wind. A couple of men whistled and laughed at her from a shady corner, but she waggled the two middle fingers of one hand at them, offending them enough that they shut up. Usually, she would have just walked by with a cringe to let them think their actions had had the desired effect, but tonight she needed to focus.

Fear still flowed through their connection at the back of her mind, as did pain. The unicorn was moving, so it had escaped whatever had hurt it, but Adren wasn't sure how to get to it before it entered the town. As far as she could tell, going down the street would lead her in the right direction. Even if it didn't, she remembered that it ended right at the forest on the edge of the town, at a place not too far from her camp. Perhaps she could direct the unicorn with her movement, keep it away from the humans as it followed her.

A lamplighter had arrived at the far end of the street and now he worked his way towards Adren, his process rhythmic as he moved from lamp to lamp. She shivered when she saw him and refused to be comforted by the glow. All it ever did was give movement to the shadow.

The unicorn's emotions dulled while Adren neared the lamplighter, down to a more manageable anxiety. It slowed and its path meandered. Adren's shoulders relaxed, only to tighten again as she passed by the lamplighter. He nodded, but she did not return the gesture. She hated him, his calm, the hiss of gas as his flame caught, the smell of rain on the air. Her hatred made the unicorn's emotions unsteady. They clashed through her, a reminder to calm herself, to keep the unicorn from unbalance. To focus on its wellbeing and the fact that it was out of danger first and foremost. Before long, its turmoil smoothed back to normal. Adren muttered a quick prayer of thanks and headed to her camp, knowing the unicorn would do the same.

Chapter Two

Of course, by "head to camp" Adren meant "stop by the lord's mansion first." She may have broken into his vault, but a mansion was another matter. And a different building. It required different information.

As darkness filled the sky, drizzle came down, misting the air more than falling. The glow of the gas lamps became ghostly with it. Adren pressed her lips together and put her hood up. She hated getting her hair wet almost as much as she hated not being able to see the stars because of the illumination. Still, as she appraised the building before her, she had to admit that the lamps made her task easier.

Three stories and spread across an area at least four times the size of the barn she'd hidden in earlier, not to mention the space taken by the garage, the mansion's sheer size gave Adren pause. Even supposing Lord Watorej had hidden the sealskin there, finding it would prove a chore. But first she would have to get inside. She stared up at the eaves, the sloping roof, the intricately carved beasts perched on its corners. Her original thought had been to climb to the roof while invisible and then enter through a window which, now that she thought about it, would have been a terrible idea. Saintsall, was it a terrible idea. There was no way she would be able to remain invisible long enough for that, and then there she would be, in full view of anyone who happened to walk by, the sealskin suddenly become the last of her priorities.

The garage door opened and a man exited, his shape silhouetted against the light from the lamps inside.

"Close it up when you're ready, then," he shouted into the garage, "but give that thing a chance to air out first. You don't want to be breathing it all night."

There came a muffled reply and the man went down the street away from Adren, whistling as he did. She wondered if the garage stayed open during the day. Once the man had gone from sight, she crept to the door and, upon reaching it, turned invisible and headed inside.

On the outside, the garage's modern design blended well with the more traditional architecture of the rest of the mansion. Past the door, however, all pretense of tradition disappeared. Adren tiptoed between the naked inner wall and one of the lines of motorized carts, their wood and metal painted a grotesque melange of colours. It was enough to give her a headache.

A loud clang echoed from the far corner of the garage, followed by a curse. Although it hadn't startled her enough for her to lose hold of her invisibility, Adren hid behind a cart and dropped the magic for a moment of rest before resuming it and passing a corner.

Halfway down the second wall, her nose wrinkled at a burnt odour emanating from the far corner. The smell only grew as she approached. She hoped she would get used to it before it started to interfere with her concentration.

There came a crack as something broke, a wordless yell close on its heels. Something flew though the air, banging against one of the carts as it went, and landing only a short distance from Adren. After a pause, the yeller sighed and came towards her. She froze, her breath slow and quiet. The yeller stopped, his shoes scraped the ground one at a time, and then nothing.

"Ah!" The voice sounded familiar, but Adren couldn't place it. It was masculine, definitely, and had cracked at the end, so she guessed it was a boy in the middle of adolescence. Her chest was tight from holding the magic, so she peered above the carts, standing on tip-toe to see where this boy was. At first, she saw no one, but then came the scrape of shoes again and his head rose over one of the carts. It was the same boy who had climbed the ladder and found her in the barn. Dirt and grease smudged his face, the freshest grease glinting in the lamplight as he turned and stared at Adren. She waited for his gaze to pass over her, or for him to walk away, but he did neither. Instead, his eyes widened and his mouth opened as his expression turned from annoyance to surprise. This unnerved Adren so much that she had to remind herself that the boy couldn't possibly see her. He must have noticed something behind her.

"Holy hell," said the boy, "what are *you* doing here?"

Adren's gut squeezed. He should not be able to see her. Could not. The magic hadn't slipped the entire time he'd seen her. She glanced back to see if there was anything that would explain this, but could only find an empty wall.

The boy squinted. "You *are* the one who broke into my lord's vault and then hid in my barn, right? Because I don't think there's anyone else around here with fairy glamour."

Adren dropped behind the cart. Her breathing quickened, near to hyperventilation, and she could feel her heart trying to pound its way out of her chest.

Sweet saints, he should not be able to see her.

"Wait!" said the boy. Soon after came a crash and a grunt of pain, then footsteps coming closer to her.

In the back of her mind, Adren could feel the unicorn respond to her fear, and its resolve to help. Any moment now, it would try to act. She wanted to calm down, but reason had left her. Blood pounded in her ears, the unicorn's madness burned within her, and she grabbed onto the wildness for strength. She let go of the invisibility and stood just as the boy reached her. He stopped a few paces away and Adren took the moment to lunge at him. As she did, he backed away, hands lifted, which she took to mean he wanted to avoid conflict.

Good.

Adren reached out with one arm and wrapped it around his neck. She sidestepped to come around behind him. Once there, she grabbed her other elbow and pressed his head with her free hand. Bent over and off balance, he tried to push her away. His movements became more frantic as she squeezed his neck, but she held fast, counting as she did.

"One, two, three, four…" the boy panicked at her voice and kept trying to push her arms, not realizing that his own chin kept her hold secure. "…five, six, seven, eight…" his movements slowed and his strength waned. "Nine…" the boy had stopped moving. Adren let go at once and dashed out of the garage. It wouldn't take him long to wake, and she couldn't afford to have him see where she went.

As she ran, she felt the unicorn's concern fade and its focus return to its hurt. She wished her fear could leave so quickly.

The moon had risen by the time Adren returned to camp. The gentle radiance could not keep all the dark at bay, but it could soften the edges, make silver out of cedar and ferns. Adren uncovered her pack by this light, taking from her pockets the dye, the fabric, the money, and removing them to their respective places. Then she took out her small store of wood and lit a fire. The flames hissed and spat, sending strange shadows through the trees before they settled into a comfortable red-orange.

Adren was about to put another log on when she heard rustling in the bush. She froze, the hairs on the back of her neck rising. Only her eyes moved as she searched the underbrush. There wasn't much in this forest, old as it was, but the spots that *had* grown between the trunks could hide someone with ease.

The rustle came again, this time accompanied by an equine the colour of the moon, and Adren relaxed. Of course it was the unicorn. That boy couldn't have woken in time to find her.

Red made an awful contrast against the white along the unicorn's flank and hindquarters where gashes, too deep and regularly spaced to have come from mere branches or thorns, marred its hide. The unicorn's anxiety shivered in the back of

Adren's mind even as the unicorn shivered in front of her. She had expected this. Terrible as it was, she had expected this.

"Oh, come here," she said as she stepped forward and wrapped her arms around its neck. Its anxiety dissolved at her touch, leaving behind only contentment. She stroked it until the tension in its muscles had ebbed away to nothing, then she kissed it at the base of its horn and stepped back to inspect.

At the unicorn's rate of healing, the wounds weren't serious, but would still benefit from some basic measures to protect against infection. Adren pulled a jar of salve from her pack and applied it with care to the wounds. The salve stung, and the unicorn flinched. Adren could feel the pain, but she gritted her teeth and remained calm for the unicorn's sake. It echoed her.

The first time she had done this, she had pressed too hard on the unicorn's wounds, and it had fled. By the time she had found it again, it had new wounds and would not let her near it. She had had to wait until it fell asleep before she could treat it and, by then, dirt had been rubbed into the raw flesh. It had taken a long time to clean and bandage everything. So now, she kept her touch as soft as possible, and her emotions as still as she was capable. The latter was the most difficult. It pained Adren to see the unicorn like this, with the consequences of its madness most clear. She didn't know where it went and what it encountered that attacked it and she didn't know why it kept rushing to these places where she could neither stop nor protect it, but she knew that no sane creature would act in such a way.

Her fingers brushed against silvery scars as she worked, yet another reminder of all the unicorn had lost. Or perhaps had never had, but Adren didn't want to believe that. While she had not met another unicorn, she knew they were wise, intelligent, and powerful. They should be able to understand speech and communicate. They should be beautiful and strong without acting like mere animals. Their healing should leave no mark.

After so many years, it was clear that the others could not help this one, or else they would have come. They may have, before it had been with Adren. Healers by nature, they would have known if one of their own was ill. They would have done all they could to bring it back to wholeness. But, with this one, their power had not been enough. Perhaps they had left the unicorn with her so that she would go into the human places and navigate their shades of deceit to find the treasure they hid. Much as she hated humans, they did tend to collect knowledge about all they came across, and so it was with them she had the best chance of finding a cure, if one existed.

Adren shook her head as she wiped the last of the salve onto the unicorn's hide. Of course there was a cure. She couldn't doubt that. Not now, not ever.

The unicorn lay down, its pain faded down to a level they both could ignore. After she retrieved some dried meat from her pack and tended the fire, Adren joined it. It put its head in her lap, sighing. This made eating awkward, with the horn jutting up in front of Adren, but she was used to it. She sometimes missed the more subtle of the unicorn's emotions, especially if something contradictory held her attention, and this action confirmed for her that the unicorn was truly at peace.

With a snap from the fire, flecks of bright ash shot into the air and went out before they touched anything. Lighting it had been unnecessary, as the night remained warm. She had gone through the trouble mostly for the ritual of it, which soothed her.

"And it's nice to look at," she said to the unicorn after swallowing the last of her food.

With the warmth before her and the unicorn behind, Adren slipped toward the border between reality and dreams.

"There once was a girl in a big house with many pretty dresses," she said, hardly aware of what she said or why. The words made a nice counterpoint to the wind in the canopy of cedar, and that was enough. "She would dance in them all the time, twirling the skirts this way and that. It was silly, but she loved it. She loved it and would do it every day to make everyone smile and, so long as she could dance, there was nothing wrong in the world. Nothing at all…"

Adren woke with a start. The fire burned lower than before,

and the unicorn was no longer behind her. Emotions boiled within the back of her mind, threatening to burst. The unicorn's tail flicked in her face and she heard the undergrowth shift as its hooves danced. She turned to see it on its feet, horn lowered and pointed out of the clearing. Only a few steps away stood a figure. Adren rose for a better look. It was the boy.

"How did you find us?" she asked. Her hostility fed into the unicorn. It started to charge, but the boy lashed out with magic that bruised the unicorn's skin in an instant. Pain flooded through both the unicorn and Adren. The unicorn faltered. It shied away, but kept its horn pointed at him. Anger had turned to rage and now it wanted violence.

The boy attacked again with magic, and Adren saw him pull out a knife as he did so. The unicorn screamed, ready to kill, and the boy's stance became more stable. He would not be able to withstand the unicorn, but his magic would do a great deal of damage before he died, and Adren didn't want the unicorn to sustain any more injury. Neither did she want to deal with the people who would come looking for the boy later.

The unicorn tensed, about to charge. Adren leapt forward. She grabbed it by the neck, doing all she could to remain stoic. The boy's eyes narrowed as he raised his knife. Despite herself, Adren's throat closed.

"Put that away!" she yelled at the boy, keeping her grip on the unicorn tight. It strained to be free, but had not yet lost itself enough to ignore her. The boy stared. "Put it away, or I won't be able to keep the unicorn back!" Adren smoothed her emotions again and pressed against the unicorn. She hoped her calm would transfer and pacify the creature before it could act.

With a frown, the boy put away his knife. He took a step back and held up his hands.

The unicorn shook, bewildered. Its desire to kill rang through their connection, hot as a bright coal and taut as a bowstring. Adren pressed her head into its neck and stroked it.

"Don't hurt him," she whispered, her voice steady and gentle. She began to hum. The melody was sweet and simple,

33

and it always worked to soothe the unicorn. Adren regretted that the boy could hear, but there was nothing to be done. The unicorn relaxed as it loosened its grip on rage—loosened, loosened, loosened, and let go. Both of its ears flicked towards her as it recognized the song. When it was more at peace, Adren also let go with a caress and stood as tall as she could next to it, one hand on its shoulder.

"It lets you touch it?" The boy gaped.

"How did you get here?" The fact that he could both see through her invisibility and use magic hinted at an explanation, but Adren couldn't yet be sure.

He shrugged. "I followed the trail."

"Like a hunter would?" Because paved roads and mossy ground were so terribly prone to showing off footprints.

"Not exactly... What are you doing all the way out here?" The boy then looked at the unicorn, his expression sheepish.

"How did you find us?" Adren demanded. "If you lie, I'll know." Well, sometimes she could. As far as she could tell, the ability was tied to her connection with the unicorn but, unlike that magic, this one was inconsistent, or consistent in a way she hadn't discovered. Of course, she wasn't going to tell *him* that.

"I have the Sight." The boy hesitated. "I'm the seventh son of a seventh son. It's why I could see through your glamour."

He was a bad liar. Adren didn't need a truth sense to tell her that. Anyone with an elementary knowledge of magic not based on superstition would know being the seventh son of anything did nothing for a person. That, and his ears were turning red. There were only two possible reasons for his magic, in order of likelihood: either he had fairy blood or someone with magic had tampered with him earlier in his life. Adren kept her expression neutral.

"So, you can see through magic. How does that help?"

"Don't you know?" His eyes widened and his mouth clamped shut. With crossed arms, he continued: "I mean... with your glamour, I thought you might be a fairy, and they know about these things."

"Well, I'm not. And stop calling it glamour. It makes you sound stupid." They paused. The red of the boy's ears spread to his face. He glanced at the fire.

"Could I sit down?"

"You're thinking of staying?"

"No. But I came here on purpose, and I'm not going to leave just because someone tries to frighten me off. I wouldn't come just to run away." The boy's posture straightened as he spoke. His arms dropped to his sides and his voice deepened with the last sentence. These changes seemed to Adren to be unconscious, which fascinated her. She wondered what there was behind these words that affected him so strongly.

The unicorn headed back to the fire and lay down. If it felt that safe with the boy around, then Adren supposed she could lower her guard a bit, but only because she was sure he wasn't fully human. And only until she decided what to do with him.

"Come and sit," she said. He obeyed. Once settled, he spoke.

"I can sometimes see magic and feel when something or someone with magic is nearby, and I can usually track it down, too, if I pay attention. That's how I found you. But maybe it was the unicorn, if you're not a fairy." His forehead wrinkled.

"Sometimes? Usually?" Adren kept her tone normal, but she was thinking of the sealskin and the magic jewel inside it.

"It's patchy," said the boy, shrugging. "If I get distracted, I don't notice it. And if I think too hard about it, then I lose it. I have to relax to see it and feel it best, I think. So, yeah. I can usually find magic things, but it takes a while most times."

Patchy as his ability was, Adren wondered whether it would be worth working with him. Would he even want to help her? She didn't need him, per se, but she wanted to keep him an ally for as long as possible. After all, he had sought her out...

"Are you human, then?" he asked.

Adren grimaced. "Yes." Mostly. Maybe. Not really. It was closer than changeling, at any rate.

"But how can you use glam..." The boy gulped. "How can you make yourself, uh, seem invisible if you're human?"

"I just can."

The boy opened his mouth again, but Adren held up a hand. He kept interrupting her thoughts, and she was about to lose the question she wanted to ask. An owl hooted nearby, making the boy jump, but otherwise he remained still. They sat like that for a while, long enough for the unicorn to fall asleep. A fog fell over the connection between her and it until all she could feel was the fact of its presence and nothing more. What had she been wanting to ask? Ah! Yes. That.

"Why did you try to find me?" The boy shrugged. Adren wished he would stop doing that.

"I was curious. I wanted to know who you were and why you'd break into my lord's vault. And his garage. Why would a fairy do that? But you're not a fairy, and now I'm confused. Why were you there?"

"I needed the money."

"But why the garage, then, if you already had what you needed? I don't understand."

The sense of truth, like the taste and smell of honeysuckle, came to Adren so strongly that she could barely breathe. How naive was this boy that he didn't even consider simple greed? Anyone else would have and dismissed her as driven by such. She chose not to answer. The boy didn't seem to notice. He only stared into the fire and continued:

"When I heard the officers shouting, I went outside and saw them run onto the street. They looked around, then a few went past my house, and the others came behind and searched everything. I asked what was going on, and they explained. When I saw some in the barn, I thought they would go right for the ladder, but they went by it like they didn't even see it. After they'd left—"

"Get on with it," said Adren.

"What?"

"You have a point. Get to it."

"Oh. I guess... when I saw you I figured you were the thief, and I didn't understand why you'd stolen. You looked like... like

36

a ghost or something ethereal. I get why you changed it, but I was so curious. I wanted to figure out what you were—"

"You thought I was a fairy." Gods in hell. Did he really need so many words? It was a wonder he got anything done.

"Only because of the... the magic. But when I tried feeling out what you were, I couldn't find it. It just felt... broken."

Adren shivered. They needed to get off this thought, and they needed to do it now. It was clear she wouldn't be able to be rid of this boy. But what to do with him?

"Let me help you," the boy said.

"Excuse me?"

"Let me help you. I'm sure I could do something, and I don't think you're really after anything bad. I don't think you're like that. And maybe, with my help, you won't have to steal." He rubbed his nose.

Well. It wasn't anything Adren hadn't already thought. Except the not having to steal part. She would definitely have to steal. There was no question about that. But how much of the truth could she reveal without putting the unicorn in danger? If the boy had only been human, Adren would have lied and been done with it, but she was almost sure he was part fairy, and magical creatures deserved better than that.

"Lord Watorej stole something from someone in town and I was trying to get it back." There. No lie. Just a lot of truth.

"More than just the money?" The boy raised his eyebrows. Adren crossed her arms.

"The money is for my own purposes. They want something magic that's held in a sealskin, but I don't know where the skin is." She paused. "You can help me find it."

"It's in a... sealskin." Lines appeared on his forehead.

"I wouldn't lie to you."

"Why would someone store something in a sealskin?"

"Saints! Will you just give me an answer?" Adren's outburst was loud enough that the unicorn stirred in its sleep.

"I'll help you. Do you have a plan?"

"No." The garage could work as an entrance point, but the

boy wouldn't be able to help her during the day. He didn't seem capable of deceiving the man he worked with. And Adren didn't want to break in during the night, which was when everyone expected thieves. They would be on the lookout. That, and Adren disliked making plans in the evening. She needed her sleep.

"Helpful." The boy grinned and Adren glared at him. He looked mildly terrified. Then: "I think I have an idea."

"What?"

"I'd have to find out if it's even possible first. Come by my house in the morning and, if it'll work, I can tell you what it is."

Adren raised an eyebrow. "And if it won't work?"

"Um. I don't know. I guess we'll just have to figure it out. Maybe come up with a few ideas before we meet, just in case?" He shrugged.

She sighed. "Fine. Make sure you're around when I come. And awake."

"Will do. See you then." The boy got up to leave, but Adren spoke and he stopped.

"Are you sure you want to help me steal from your lord?" Fairy blood or not, he still had human in him, and he had only used words. It was far too easy to make words hide the truth.

He paused. Nodded to himself.

"Yes."

The sweetness of honeysuckle spread over Adren's tongue and she silently thanked whoever or whatever decided when the magic worked. At some point, she would to learn how to predict it. Until then, she was grateful that it happened at all.

"What's your name?"

"Excuse me?" The question had so rarely been asked of her that it surprised her.

"What's your name?"

"Adren." The word felt rusty in her mouth, as if her lips were unpractised at forming it.

"It's a pleasure to meet you," said the boy as he made a small bow. "My name's Nadin."

Chapter Three

"Tell me this is a joke." Adren crossed her arms and glared at Nadin. He shrugged. "And stop doing that. It's monotonous."

"No. To both." He shrugged exaggeratedly.

"I won't do it." The plan made her want to retch.

"Then what's *your* plan?"

Adren thought quickly. "We'd break in. Or you'd help me get in. We'd find the sealskin."

"Well, this is me helping you get in. Unless you can keep yourself invisible the whole time you search the mansion yourself, because I won't be helping you during the day. You don't realize how many people there are in the building then."

"So get me in at night," said Adren through gritted teeth.

"I don't have a key. The door locks on my side."

"Break the door down."

Nadin stared at her for a moment, his mouth hanging open. Then he lifted his arms to the sky with a sound of exasperation and threw the livery onto the table. He had brought it from the mansion before they met, after arranging for Adren to work at the mansion that day. The idea was that, come evening, she would let him in from the garage and he would use his magic to help her find the jewel in the sealskin.

"I don't know how you managed to make away with Lord

Watorej's money." He folded his arms. "Look. The door to the inside of the house can't be broken down if I want to keep my job. Anyone with sense would know I was the one to let you in, because I'm the only one in the garage at night. We couldn't even make it seem like you managed to get past me because I know how to get around the mansion and you don't."

"I can turn invisible."

"Yes, but I can't. If we're going to work together, then we *both* have to get in undetected. If anyone knew I'd helped you break in, I'd lose my job, go to prison, and never be able to get another job here for the rest of my life." By the end of the last sentence, Nadin's face was red and he blinked back tears. Odd.

"Saints!" Adren exploded after a pause. "Why do you care? Go to another town and get a job there."

"I can't just—"

"Why not?"

"Because I grew up here! This is my home, where my friends are, where I've been all my life! Who in their right mind would throw that away for the sake of one event? And what should I do at the next town if something like this comes around again?" His expression turned to horror when he saw that she was unconcerned. "Is that what you do all the time? Just show up somewhere, turn everyone against you, and then leave?"

"None of that matters to me." Adren stuffed her hands in her pockets and clenched them into fists.

"Like hell. There are only so many towns and cities in the world. If you make them all hate you, then you'll never have a home. Don't you want somewhere to call home?"

Adren gave a dry laugh. "I don't need towns or cities. Get back to the plan." Nadin's words had stung, more than she liked to admit, so her words came out harshly, but she wasn't about to take them back. He didn't know enough to understand her position and she wasn't about to recount a history. They had a jewel to steal. Now was not the time to get sidetracked.

"Why?" he asked. The tone was harmless. The word was not.

She met his gaze with a deliberate motion, her eyes blue ice.

A dozen possible replies ran through her mind, words which would push his question aside and move to the task at hand. They all fled the chill growing at her centre, a chill which slowed her words to make them wintry clear.

"Because I hate humans. Gods in hell, Nadin, you think I want a home with them? I would rather die than spend the rest of my life in a town full of those filth." Nadin reacted as if he'd been punched in the gut.

"I'm glad to know that's how you feel," he said, more bitterly than she had expected. "Enjoy hating yourself so thoroughly."

They faced each other, Nadin trembling, Adren still as death.

A woman called Nadin's name weakly from the second floor. He headed up the stairs, then paused at the top. "Don't go. I still want to help you." A door creaked as he opened it and entered the room, speaking to its occupant in soothing tones.

She looked askance at the livery. Its bright red silk reminded her of the dye shop owner and her put-on cheerfulness. She picked it up and tried to find something wrong with it.

Did she hate herself? She mouthed Nadin's words with a sneer. What a ridiculous accusation. Even if, saints forbid, she were part human, she clearly wasn't wholly so. Neither was Nadin, but he'd grown up among them, so she supposed it was only natural he would follow their lead and pay sole attention to appearance. His hurt on their behalf was also reasonable, although the strength of his attachment surprised Adren. But to accuse her of hating herself? Gods. The nerve.

At any rate, Nadin cared about keeping his job and the favour of humans, and Adren had to admit his plan was well thought out, if distasteful. Could she endure a whole day of serving in a mansion full of humans? She hoped to all the saints in heaven that she could. Nadin's skills were too valuable to ignore, and he too hazardous to her success to cast aside. The unicorn needed this cure and it didn't matter whose plan Adren followed or how much as she hated it, so long as it worked. Besides, she couldn't find any reason to reject the livery.

Nadin descended the stairs, face drawn and steps heavy.

"I'll do it," Adren told him. He nodded, then stopped and narrowed his eyes.

"You're agreeing to my plan? I thought you didn't… I mean, I thought you… I mean—" he took a breath. "Thank you."

"I'm not doing it for you," said Adren, observing as Nadin started to shrug, then stopped himself. He opened his mouth, closed it, then glanced up the stairs.

"Well, change into the livery and we can go," he said finally. "I hadn't thought you wouldn't like the plan, so we're running later than I told them to expect."

Adren rolled her eyes. "Of course. Where do I change?"

"Um." Nadin blushed and started up the stairs. "Just… tell me when you're done. We don't have an extra room." He disappeared onto the top floor.

With a sigh, Adren removed her coat. As she changed, she checked on the unicorn. Thankfully it only felt content, without even a hint of the kind of curiosity that forewarned trouble. The unicorn had gone far enough away that she was worried she wouldn't be able to tell if it were in trouble. Strong as their connection was, the unicorn's emotions became faint with enough distance. It was possible that it could wander so far she wouldn't be able to feel anything from it, but the idea made her shiver. She and the unicorn had always had some sense of each other for as long as she could remember, some intuition. This transfer of feeling that had unfurled during Pider's betrayal had only brought what they already had to conscious awareness and, uncomfortable as it could be, Adren had grown used to it. She didn't want to know what it was like to be alone.

The livery fit well, though a bit wide in the shoulders and the waist, and the design wouldn't impede movement should things go bad and they needed to run or fight. Even the best plans fell apart when enacted. It was only a matter of when and how. She fastened the belt with a jerk and then removed her money from her coat to put it in the robe's inner pocket.

"Nadin!"

When he returned, his face was calm enough, but he

didn't seem to know what to do with his hands. Adren couldn't tell if his agitation resulted from the impending task or the woman upstairs, and Nadin didn't offer an explanation. He only led her out of the house and locked the door before they started on their way to the mansion.

The smell of meat cooking wafted down the streets, carried by the same wind that caused intermittent dust devils in the alleys as Adren and Nadin passed. A group of children played with a ball at a crossing, chanting to each other and screaming as they ran in convoluted patterns, their antics supervised by an elderly woman who sat on a bench in front of one of the houses. Her eyelids drooped, but she did not hesitate to scold one of the younger girls for nearly tripping a boy with the ball, or the boy when he tried to trip the girl back only a moment later.

Nadin picked up speed, and Adren's shorter legs had to work to match his stride. His jaw clenched each time they passed someone on the street, but he nodded in greeting to those that noticed him and Adren. Occasionally, one or two people on horseback would ride by, the horses' hooves clattering on the cobblestone that paved this part of town, and the two of them would have to slow down and get out of the way, since riders never made any attempt to keep from hitting anyone on foot.

While Adren preferred excess silence to excess speech, Nadin's actions made this particular silence so strained that she could almost feel the tension coming off him like steam. She wanted to say something about the matter, but decided to let him stew in his own thoughts. It wouldn't be hard to ignore.

A motorized cart roared past, as oblivious to anything on the road as the riders had been, and a few people had to make a dash to get out of its way. Adren caught a glimpse of the man driving it, his expression gleeful. As the cart passed by, she could hear the shrieking and giggling of several young women, their noise peaking each time it swerved or came close to hitting someone.

"That's Lord Watorej," said Nadin after the cart had gone from sight. "He likes to show off for the daughters of the richer families in town, since he's one of the only people here who

43

has those carts. He's constantly damaging them by starting or stopping too fast, or making sloppy turns and hitting things with it. At least he hasn't hit any people yet. I make sure the carts' engines go fast enough to thrill him, but not so fast that people can't get out of the way when they hear him coming." He gave a small smile, then fell silent again. A woman called out, trying to sell them fruit she claimed to have picked earlier that morning, but Nadin shook his head and they walked past.

At the next crossing, he spoke again. "My mother—the one who called me upstairs—she's been sick for years. I've tried everything I could possibly think of, saving up the money to pay for the things I couldn't afford right away, but nothing's worked. No one can tell me what's wrong with her. Whether they look for magic, disease, or poison, whether they look inside or out, they can't find anything. And it's only been getting worse. Until recently, her mind remained as healthy as it had always been, but it's begun to go as well. You may not understand the comfort of staying in the same place your entire life, but you have to at least be able to imagine what it's like to take care of someone who can hardly take care of themselves, to be responsible for their life because no one else can or will. That's why I can't risk losing my job or this town, more than anything else."

Adren felt as if a knife had been shoved into her heart and twisted. At first, when she tried to speak, the back of her throat contorted and refused to let anything past, and her tongue glued itself to the top of her mouth. She swallowed, trying to loosen the muscles, hoping that most of this came from the overwhelming sense of truth his words had triggered.

"I u-understand." Her mouth clammed shut as her heart flooded over. More tried to force itself through her lips, but she did not dare say any of it. The unicorn was her business and no one else's. If anyone knew that it was vulnerable, she knew only too well what they would try to do. After her encounter with Pider, Adren had only learned more about the depravity of humans, and the things some would do to unicorns made her retch. That particular incident, had been the first, though, and

44

had given her such terrible nightmares that she barely slept for a week, and then only when she was too exhausted to fight it. What she had learned later was even worse. She would still wake in the middle of some nights, covered with sweat and fresh from a dream where Pider hacked off the unicorn's horn with a sword. A tremor ran through her body before she could stop it. Nadin glanced at her with concern in his eyes.

"Is something wrong?"

Adren shook her head, but couldn't keep her expression neutral. Tears built up behind her eyes, so she stopped and shut her lids tight. She heard Nadin stop as well.

Never, as far back as she could remember, had she met anyone in a situation so like her own. Oh, saints, how she wished it was safe to tell him. A memory flashed into her mind of a little girl running up to her father to whisper a secret in his ear, her fair hair bright against his black clothing. Her mind snatched at it like someone dying of thirst would snatch at rain, but it fled before she could grasp the pictures, and all that remained was an ache.

The unicorn had started an approach, worried for her, and she tried to calm herself down. She didn't understand how Nadin's words had brought about such a rush of emotion, but neither did she want to, for fear of that rush never ending.

"Can I help?" His boots scraped against the road as he stepped forward and, when Adren opened her eyes, she could see his hand reaching towards her shoulder. She recoiled.

"Don't touch me!"

Several passersby gave curious glances, but Nadin seemed not to notice. He pulled his arm back, but concern remained on his face. "We need to keep going."

Adren resumed walking, and Nadin followed suit, but her attention remained on returning the pain inside of her to its hiding place. Slowly, as she calmed, the unicorn's worry turned to puzzlement, then to peace. Once she had returned to normal, it stopped coming for her.

At the end of the street stood the mansion, looking even

larger now that Adren saw it in the daylight. The blue roof and red-framed windows stared down on her in condescension. Nadin had been right about the amount of people on the grounds during the day. Aside from the expected security officers on guard, she counted at least five gardeners tending to the flowers, shrubs, and trees, three mechanics taking a break in the garage, and four maids, two scrubbing the roof and two keeping an eye on the ladders while washing the ground-level windows. While breaking in by herself wouldn't have been impossible, it still would have been very, very difficult. Nadin grinned at her.

"Lord Watorej has a lot of money, and he likes to spend it," he said. "It's a point of personal pride for him that he has more of everything than anyone thinks he needs, even if he doesn't do anything important with it. And it has to be cleaned constantly. That's the third time this week the roof's been washed."

"That explains the job opening."

"You're glad you agreed to my plan, aren't you?"

"Barely." Not only would she work for a human, but even humans considered the work meaningless. Adren was certain that hell had a quarter exactly like this and, if she had any say in the matter, people like Lord Watorej would go there after death.

Nadin rapped on the door with the gold knocker shaped like a ring held in the forepaws of an otter. After a moment, a footman wearing ornate livery opened the door and stood to the side to let a woman greet Adren and Nadin.

"My Lady Watorej," said Nadin with a bow, and Adren clumsily copied him. The lady smiled.

"Hello to you both." Her gaze didn't meet theirs, appearing to look both inwards and far away at the same time. When she gestured to let them in, she moved as if half-dreaming and nearly knocked over a lamp before the footman placed a hand on her shoulder to stop her. Adren had seen people like this in cities, people who tried to escape the world through the use of potions or magic that distracted their attention and emotions. The lady didn't seem as far gone as some, but Adren knew that, given time, she wouldn't be able to do even this, being too lost in her own reality. She glanced at Nadin, wondering if he understood the lady's condition, but he was smiling back.

"My lady, this is Adren, the replacement for Eneli." The lady nodded. Adren nodded back.

"She is more than just a replacement, methinks."

Adren's heart skipped a beat as much at that last word as the rest of the sentence, and she saw Nadin's Adam's apple bob. The footman raised an eyebrow at them, but he kept his mouth shut.

The lady closed her eyes and shook her head. When she opened them, her gaze was sharp and clear. She took in their faces, looking back and forth as if she had only just seen them.

"I'm sorry, what did I say? My mind is always a little fuzzy in the mornings, and some of the things that come out of my mouth are half-mad. Oh, and are you the replacement Nadin said he was bringing? For... for..."

"Eneli," Nadin supplied. Adren nodded, dumbfounded by such an abrupt switch. This was so unlike anything she'd ever seen that she almost reconsidered her original assessment.

"Eneli. Such a lovely name. Such a sweet girl, too. But I'm glad we were able to find a replacement so fast, thanks to Nadin. My husband would not like to hear that we have fewer servants than before, especially after that robbery from his vault."

"Has anyone found the thief?" Nadin asked, more smoothly than Adren had thought him capable. The lady shook her head.

"I don't think so, but they should turn up soon. The gossip runs that they are quite distinctive in appearance." This made Adren want to laugh. Dyeing her hair and skin was such an obvious method of disguise that she could never get used to people who didn't consider it. "Oh, but I am keeping you from your work. I'm sorry. I trust you know your way, Nadin?"

"Yes, my lady." They farewelled each other and Nadin led Adren through the house. She paid little attention to where they were going, choosing instead to search as discreetly as possible for potential hiding places for the sealskin. By the time they stopped, she had counted more than two dozen paintings, a handful of tapestries, and more furniture than was decent. In addition were two grand staircases—one of which they went up and then back down as Nadin temporarily lost track of where he was going—under which could be secret doors. Of course, these were only the obvious locations on the first floor of the mansion. From what she could see through the windows, the estate contained a few more buildings any of which could contain, secreted away in some corner, the sealskin and the jewel inside of it. She had also noticed a regal grandfather clock in a room on the second floor. Who knew how a clever person might make use of *that?* Adren began to despair at the thought of, even with the help of Nadin's magic, weeks of working for this detestable lord before their nighttime searches uncovered anything useful.

"I didn't warn you about the lady," Nadin said, hand on a doorknob. "She's only like that for most of the morning, and sometimes a little in the evening. And a bit at night, when she sleepwalks. From what I hear, it used to be worse. When she first came to live here, she really was half-mad and a little violent, too. But she's a lot better, and has been improving every year."

Adren raised an eyebrow. "When she sleepwalks?"

Nadin's expression turned sheepish. "*If* she sleepwalks. It's not every night." He blushed.

"I'm so very glad you thought to mention this detail now," said Adren flatly. "Will someone go after her when she does?"

"She might not tonight."

"I don't trust chance." Though she hated to plan beforehand, Adren found it fruitful to act as if the worst possibility would occur, and then take the opportunity given if it didn't.

"No one will come after her. She just wanders around the house, talking to herself. Up until a few years ago, she would tear whole rooms apart, but that was a while ago. If she finds us—" The footman walked past, looking down his nose at the two of them. Once he was out of earshot, Nadin continued, whispering this time. "If she finds us, you'll have to go invisible, and I'll convince her to leave. She's come down to the garage before while I was working, so I know how to deal with her."

"You had better."

Chapter Four

Adren's chance to search the mansion didn't come until late in the day. The housekeeper was a suspicious woman and organized it such that Adren had constant supervision. And then, sometime after the midday meal, she burst into the room that Adren and two others were cleaning—or, more accurately, the room that Adren was cleaning to distract herself from the gossip session the others had stopped to enjoy. She was beginning to wonder if they'd notice if she just stood up and left.

"You!" The housekeeper pointed at Adren. "I need extra hands." Adren, glad for the change, went to the door. Just before she closed it, the housekeeper stuck her head in to glare at the two inside with stone-hard eyes. "I'll deal with you later." Then she led Adren through the mansion at such a quick pace that Adren had to jog to keep up.

They raced to the third floor, the housekeeper pushing past anyone who got in the way, then up a ladder and into an attic. Inside, Lady Watorej knelt on the floor, dumping the contents of a wooden box and weeping. Others lay strewn around her, the items they had housed surrounding them in irregular piles.

"Where is it? I need to cover myself!" She threw one of the now-empty boxes across the room and wrapped her arms around herself, shivering.

"She's having a remission," the housekeeper told Adren. "We need to bring her to her room for treatment. Do what I do."

The housekeeper approached the lady slowly, her palms displayed. The lady didn't seem to see either of them. She stood and began to pace, rubbing her arms. A moan escaped her lips, low and sustained, turning into a scream when she stopped in the middle of the attic and clawed at her head.

"Oh, that I would ever have called you 'thou!'" she yelled at the window, her voice raw. Adren faltered at that word. Humans never used it; it was part of the dialects magical creatures used with each other. Referring to someone as 'thou' meant they were another magical being or, if they were a human, then the speaker considered them someone precious. Nadin had mentioned that the lady used to be half-mad. Had someone made her that way? Fairies might, after one had seduced her. And yet, fairy madness got worse, if it ever changed, and Nadin had assured her that the lady had been improving. Admittedly, Adren had seen little that she would consider improvement upon madness, but she had not known the lady for longer than a few hours.

"My lady, come with me," the housekeeper said as she inched ever closer.

The lady waggled her index finger and stumbled back over an upturned box. While she was distracted, the housekeeper caught Adren's eye and indicated she should come around to the right, which would trap the lady in a corner. Adren obeyed, her thoughts still occupied with the lady's condition.

If the lady were dependent on a substance that had caused her episode at the door, she might be taking it to escape the memories of what fairies had done. But then why would she have used dialect when she had greeted Adren?

"No, no, no! I shall not be tricked again!" The lady fell this time, and the housekeeper took swift advantage of this, grabbing her. She struggled against the housekeeper and nearly escaped, but Adren lent her strength and they calmed the flailing together. As they did, a man's voice called from the floor below.

"Klar, you need any help getting her down?"

"Yes. Wait." The housekeeper braced herself as she and Adren tried to gently pull the lady towards the ladder. She balked, shaking. Then she froze and turned to Adren.

"Let not them have me always," she pleaded, eyes wild. "Let not them own me."

"I shall not," Adren responded quietly, chilled. This bit of dialect would sound merely old-fashioned to the humans, but it was enough for the lady. She relaxed and let Adren and the housekeeper take her to the ladder, climbing down without any fuss. The housekeeper followed, her motions rife with tension, but the lady did not flee. Instead she went calmly with the man, a doctor. The housekeeper stared as they left.

Saints and all the gods besides, Adren had been stupid.

"I'd usually get Eneli to help when this happened. You did well." The housekeeper's voice pulled Adren's attention away from the lady and the complication she had just introduced. "How did you manage to calm her down so well?"

"I don't know," Adren replied. The lie burned her tongue, but she dared not say the truth.

After a pause, the housekeeper cleared her throat. "Well. Back to work, then."

Adren left as quickly as she could. Her heart pounded and, try as she did to slow it, she couldn't focus. Lady Watorej was a magical creature of some kind, held captive. The servants might not know the truth, but the lord certainly did. Who else would the lady resent calling 'thou' if not him? He may have even been using the jewel he stole from the potion maker to make the lady docile, blaming her attempts at escape on madness. If the jewel could aid in the healing of true madness, it could have the ability to change the mind in other ways. Manipulating healing magic to cause harm... the idea horrified Adren.

But at least now she was alone.

She leaned back against a tapestry of a party of nobles hunting a deer. The animal's eyes were wide, but the nobles laughed, relaxed in their saddles as they drew their bows. Adren's fists shook. Her entire body shook, so much so that it took several breaths to still her muscles. What kind of man was this Lord Watorej? She pounded against the tapestry as if she could blot the noble's pointed boot out of existence. When the unicorn was cured, they would come and rescue the lady, and no one would be able to stand in their way. Gentle as unicorns were, when they fought, even dragons trembled at their rage. Adren would not rest until the deed was done. Saints help her, she would not. Her heart wrapped around the fury, turning it to the fuel of cold determination. She set to work, an ear out for any passersby in case she needed to turn invisible.

Cautious as Adren was, quick as she was to hide herself, there really were too many people in the mansion. She had just entered the library, which held the clock she had noticed that morning while Nadin had brought her through the mansion, when the footman exited. He raised an eyebrow at Adren and hurried by, muttering.

"That *boy* has such poor taste."

Adren ducked into the room and laughed silently, only to grow serious as she considered the implications of his sentence. Why Nadin had decided to help still remained a mystery, and the footman wouldn't have seen anything in Adren's actions to give rise to his statement. Nadin himself hadn't displayed that kind of interest in Adren while in her presence, but still. The idea of him having a crush on her made her uncomfortable. If the footman were right, what would Nadin do when he didn't get what he wanted?

The clock rang the hour, which caused Adren to jump. It continued its melody, oblivious. In such a large clock, there should be a door of some kind so the mechanism could be tended, but there was none she could yet see. Adren tilted her head. As the clock's announcement came to a close, she ran her hands up along the sides of its body to check for any seams too small for the eye to notice, but found none. Perhaps the top…

"Lost?"

The housekeeper stood in the doorway. Saints. The ringing must have covered her footsteps.

"Completely." This was ridiculous. Couldn't one search a mansion in peace?

After receiving directions, Adren headed to the third floor instead. She and Nadin would have time to search the clock during the night. Before then, it was clear she needed a place to hide until then. With Lady Watorej's recent actions, it was more than likely the servants would be keeping a close enough eye on her that she wouldn't go to the attic again.

As Adren neared the attic, three laundry workers carrying bedding from saints knew where passed the ladder. One of the two women dropped part of her load and the others stopped to help, giving Adren a chance to turn invisible.

"These are going to get holes in them, we've washed them so much," complained the woman, taking the dropped blankets from her companions. "Look at this! It's so thin here." She showed them the place.

"Oh, he'll just buy a new one when it's worn out," said the second woman with a shrug.

"It doesn't make sense. Why would he wear everything out so quickly only to replace it all again? It's like he's trying to destroy what he has."

The young man between them handed her the last sheet, nodded, and said, "It doesn't matter how much money he has. He can't possibly keep up with all of this. And what will we do if he goes bankrupt?"

"Another five years of this and we'll know, I'm sure," observed the first woman. All of her things returned to her arms, they continued on their way. Adren squeezed against the wall as they passed, careful not to disturb what they carried.

"I think it's all to impress the lady. She comes here and next thing you know..." The second woman's sentence was lost as they turned a corner. Adren wasn't sure what to make of that exchange. While it was possible the lord was under a curse cast by Lady Watorej upon her capture, she had not displayed any overt magic when Adren had seen her wild in the attic. She had only been searching for something 'to cover herself.'

Adren's breath caught in her throat. But no, the sealskin belonged to the potion maker. Lady Watorej must have been trying to find something else. She had to have been.

The ladder creaked as Adren stepped on it. She paused, the hairs of her neck rising. Although her magic still held, it would not do for someone to investigate the sound. The hall remained empty, so she climbed into the attic and shut the door carefully behind her. Around her stood piles of boxes, some of plain wood, others ornamented with brass or steel. She had planned on searching them until night fell, but the thought of their hinges making untoward noise now gave her pause. Invisibility still in place, she tried the lid of one of the nearer boxes. It squealed before she could open it more than a sliver, setting her teeth on edge. She put an ear to the door. Nothing, thank the saints. Well, then. She let go of her magic, resigned to the fact that she would have to wait.

She hated waiting.

The moon had risen by the time Adren found her way to the inner door of the garage. She tapped on it, cursing herself. A whole day in the mansion and she had forgotten to use any of it to locate this place. At least Nadin expected her and could, at the very least, communicate through the door when he heard her.

Someone slid a piece of paper with writing on it under the door, followed by a stubby pencil. Adren groaned and rolled her eyes. He just had to be literate. People in cities and larger towns had the annoying tendency to assume that everyone else could read and write just because *they* could. She pushed the paper back and kicked the pencil at him with great prejudice. A whispered "hell!" came from the other side of the door, followed by Nadin muttering fiercely.

"If you're going to send it back, at least write your answer on it. Then I might forgive you for hitting my shin with the point of that pencil."

"I can't read, idiot," Adren replied in a loud whisper, wishing it was possible to hiss those words.

"Adren?"

"No, I'm your fairy godmother." Oh. What if he really *did* have a fairy godmother? Adren unlocked the deadbolt and opened the door. Nadin stopped rubbing his shin and entered the mansion, closing and locking the door behind him.

"Did you find anywhere promising?" he asked. Then his eyes grew very wide as he stared over Adren's shoulder. She turned around. The footman approached, lamp in hand. The shadows it gave his face made it appear even longer than it was, long and bony. He wrinkled his nose and sniffed.

"Unless anywhere is outside the mansion, you'll find your activities most unwelcome." Nadin made sounds of extreme confusion. The footman raised an eyebrow at him. "I sleep twice at night, young man, and I take a walk around the grounds between those times. How you weren't aware of this, I have no idea. I'm only glad I decided to come this way tonight and stop these heathen actions before they even started."

For a moment, Adren's fury convinced her that the best way to get out of this situation was to argue with the footman that she and Nadin weren't lovers. Then she realized he would want to know what they were doing together instead. She sighed.

"We won't be doing it inside the mansion."

The footman gave a significant glance at the door.

"Nadin left something inside when he brought me here."

"What sort of something?"

All the saints and gods besides, she was drawing a blank.

"My wallet. See?" said Nadin, his voice steady as he showed his empty pockets. The footman looked unconvinced.

"You could have left your wallet at home when you came here now. Why would you even need it at this time of night?"

"How am I supposed to lock the garage without keys?"

The footman squinted at Nadin, holding his gaze. Common knowledge held that this could test a person's honesty, but Adren knew that all it tested was their confidence. She didn't want to bet on Nadin being a confident liar and be wrong.

"Nadin, let's just do our 'activities' right now. Seeing as he won't believe anything else from us," she took a step towards him. The footman recoiled, his lamp swinging.

"Go find your wallet. It's time I went back to sleep."

Both Adren and Nadin nodded, and the footman took off. Adren laughed. Nadin just stared at the footman's quickly receding figure, mouth open.

"What just happened?" His question only made Adren laugh even more, her sides shaking as she tried to keep silent. Funny as the result had been, Adren's laughter stemmed more from a release of the tension that had built since she had robbed the lord's vault. Oh, but the footman's face when she had made her suggestion had been too perfect. She could not deny she enjoyed getting back at him for his gossip. In the back of her mind, she felt the unicorn wake for a moment, terrified, but it soon returned her amusement and went back to sleep.

Excitement filled Adren as she thought of the cure the next day would bring, and how she would tell the unicorn this story, but she only allowed herself a moment's indulgence. She had to remain undistracted if she and Nadin were to succeed. Oh, but what a joy it would be!

"He thought we were lovers," Adren told Nadin once she had calmed enough.

"What?" His face turned a spectacular shade of red.

"Sssshh! We only have so much time. Questions later." Nadin followed as she tried to remember the way back to the attic. The mansion held deep shadows at this hour. Near the windows, all the darkness could do was obscure details, but farther away the black couldn't be held at bay. There it engulfed the surroundings, body and soul.

Aside from that place in her mind, Adren wasn't afraid of the dark, but she didn't scoff at those who were. The night could change the shape and character of a place so completely as to make it alien. Even if someone had walked a road a thousand times in the day, they would not know it once the sun had fallen, and so would fear to tread it. Light showed the world as it was, but darkness hid it, made it unknown, made the mind have to invent things to fill the gaps between the light.

But those gaps did not bring the greatest terror—that honour belonged to when the unseen and seen mixed. Darkness would twist the shapes of what a person could perceive but, when it had the power to manipulate the light, it wouldn't make those shapes unrecognizable. Instead, it would force the viewer to recognize them; it would hold their attention so that they could not hide from the horror of what they saw: that which they had known and taken for granted made into their enemy. To see with the light something they had trusted and why they had trusted it, even as the darkness revealed how false that trust had been. When the two mixed so constantly that no one had ever seen them apart, how, then, could anyone know what was true?

And if no one knew what was true, then how could they do anything but fear?

The moon shone through a window at the end of the hall as Adren stopped to remember how to get to the third floor. If the stairs from the main floor had been there, the kitchen was over there, and they were next to the window, then... then... She kneaded her fingers against her forehead, trying to recreate a map of the floor in her head. If only they could walk through walls. If only she had both hers *and* Nadin's magic.

"Anything?" she asked. Nadin scanned their surroundings.

"Up that way, I think," he said, staring to her left, at a place where the wall and ceiling met.

Adren frowned. Nadin had admitted his magic was patchy, but that didn't mean she had to like his uncertain phrasing.

Nadin grinned. "Time for a game of hot-and-cold."

"What?"

"You know, hot-and-cold." Adren shook her head. "The children's game?" Again she shook her head. Nadin sighed. "Never mind." He rubbed his hands and started down the hallway, Adren following.

They kept their footsteps soft, Adren alert to all other sounds, in case the footman wasn't the only person to prowl the mansion at night, and if the lady started sleepwalking. Would Nadin be able to detect her before she came? That depended on which magic he could see, and which the lady had.

Despite the diversity of magical creatures, there were only two kinds of magic. The first only gave abilities, like Adren's invisibility and Nadin's ability to see through it, and it was predefined and limited in scope. The second involved raw magic living inside the creature, the material from which spells could be created, or magical objects, or abilities given to another non-magical being. In living things, this living magic always came with the other, but abilities could exist in a creature without it.

Nadin had said he could find magical objects, which meant he could see the second kind, and which meant he would be able to find the jewel, but there was also a chance he could find the lady. Adren prayed she was right about the lady's magic, and that Nadin wouldn't be able to see it.

They had reached the third floor when Adren heard a door open on the floor below them, somewhere near the bottom of the stairs. She and Nadin stiffened, listening to the footsteps as they travelled away from the staircase. Before long, they faded, and the two relaxed.

"At which point they both wondered if the mysterious walker only needed to relieve themselves," whispered Nadin with a grin.

"I didn't," Adren said. Nadin shrugged as his smile fell.

"Do you know where we could go? I think I lost track of the magic."

She considered kicking him for letting the walker distract him that much, but it would have done them little good.

"This way." She went past him, having reoriented herself by this point. He muttered something to himself, but she ignored him. Conversation would only distract them further, and silence gave Adren more peace than talk ever did. Nadin could squirm all he wanted if the quiet bothered him. He would never know the beauty of a clear, ordered mind if he insisted on filling every spare inch of his life with words, but that wasn't her problem.

They had nearly reached the attic ladder when a noise came from behind. Nadin shoved her into a nearby room, closing the door and, with a thunk as his back hit the wood, stood in front of it. Adren's heart started to race. Close as the room already felt in the dark, she could swear the walls were pressing inwards, a sensation that made her skin crawl. She was about to swear at Nadin, but his voice stopped her.

"My lady."

Sweet saints. Had they walked by her without seeing?

Chapter Five

Several courses of action occurred to Adren, not the least of which was bursting through the door and out of this room. Was there a clock inside? She thought she heard a tick-tock-tick-tock from the corner, a mockery of her own heartbeat. With a deliberate breath, she tried to get herself under control. The unicorn remained asleep, off in the forest, and it needed to stay that way. Besides, forcible escape would only harm their chances at finding the sealskin. With the lady's condition being what it was, there was no way to predict how she would react to Adren's presence, and Adren wasn't in the mood to find that out. She opted for another path and pressed her ear against the door, listening intently.

"Your... lady?" a second voice said hoarsely.

"Yes, you are my lady. Lady Watorej."

"What does that mean, 'Watorej'? It cannot be my name if I know naught of what it means."

"Certainly it could. I don't know what *my* name means, but I've never held that against it. My lady, why are you here?"

"I thought the ocean had risen from the shore to carry me away, but now I perceive neither where it has gone nor if it ever came. I dearly wish for water again." The lady's voice had a singsong cadence, which Adren hoped signified sleepwalking.

"Maybe if you went back to your room, you'd find it."

"But it is my room that cages me, keeps me locked from the other half of my being." A pause. "I see your meaning. Even if the ocean came, I could not run away with it. I am naked."

Adren's breath caught. She knew now what the lady was.

"My lady, I assure you that you're not... naked. You must just be cold and wanting to return to your warm blankets."

"Mayhap, but methinks not." But her quiet footsteps indicated she had left.

Adren opened the door and left the room with a shudder. How open the hall was! She jabbed Nadin, who was staring down the hallway, in the shoulder. He rubbed it, shook his head, and focused on Adren. She pointed at the attic ladder and he followed her up.

In the attic, they set to work; Adren opened the boxes and chests as quietly as possible while Nadin checked everything for magic. Lord Watorej kept some of the strangest things. One box contained nothing but bent nails, and another held only a seashell. Nearly half the chests had one doll included among their contents, no matter what the rest was. A few chests appeared to be made of what were originally the planks of a ship, a few with barnacles stuck to them. By the light coming in from the window, Adren could make out words painted on some. And, as much as she searched with dedication, Nadin seemed distracted. He kept going through the same boxes. She had to remind him multiple times to move on to the next.

"Do any of them contain anything magical?" she asked, exasperated. He paused, cocked his head as if to listen, and then shook it. Adren could hardly believe it. They had already searched at least two dozen containers. "You were planning on telling me this when?"

He shrugged, then paused. "The lady isn't human."

"Excuse me?"

"I think she's a selkie. What she said about the ocean and being naked... I don't know why I never noticed her magic until now. I just thought she was a little out of her head. You're getting the sealskin for her, aren't you? So she can escape and turn back into a seal? And the magic thing inside of it is just that: magic." His voice was low, thoughtful.

Nadin was right, for what it was worth. Lady Watorej was a selkie. No wonder the lord had a doctor giving her treatments so that she would act human—many in this part of the country held views about what the saints taught about the intermarriage of humans and magical creatures that would create problems for his reputation. "It's not hers. Someone else owns it. I don't know where hers is." Adren readied herself for the possibility that Nadin might try to stop her. A jewel case that doubled as a decoy sealskin… Lord Watorej was more paranoid than she had expected. Or more controlling.

Nadin frowned. "But it has to be hers. Why else would Lord Watorej keep it in his mansion?"

"For the thing inside of it," Adren said through gritted teeth.

"Which is what, exactly?" Nadin crossed his arms. "I'm not going any further until you tell me what you're really doing here. There is no way I'll help you harm Lady Watorej in any way."

"But you're willing to steal from your lord?"

"You said he'd stolen it from someone else. I thought I was helping get it back to its rightful owner. What's really going on?"

Nadin may have been part fairy, but his ties to humans were close. Telling him that the unicorn was vulnerable would only open it to more harm. Especially with his mother so ill… even if she told him now and the unicorn was cured the next morning, what would stop him from finding it before then and using it against its will? But suppose he decided to wait until the unicorn was sane again and suppose that the potion maker's cure ended up being powerless, or a fake. Adren wasn't sure how well she would be able to defend the unicorn from him if he brought allies and didn't hold back with his magic.

"I don't trust you," she finally said.

Even in the shadows, Adren could see that Nadin wrestled with something. His hands had become fists, clenched until his knuckles turned white, and he chewed his lip.

"Adren, I don't want to hurt you." His eyebrows shot up and he nodded to himself. "I don't want to hurt you."

The sentiment was nice, perhaps. It was also what someone said to blame their circumstances for the eventual pain they would inflict. Or they blamed the person they hurt. The truth was that no one ever did what they didn't, on some level, want. Adren wanted to toss the statement aside, and Nadin with it, except for the sweetness that spread across her tongue.

"Do you really believe that?"

"Yes."

Was that all it was? That she could sense the truth when the person who said it also believed it, deeply? It couldn't be. It couldn't. She didn't want to trust Nadin. Not with this. She hadn't trusted anyone with this since…

But there was no other choice. She needed him on her side.

"There's a potion maker in town who needs the magic jewel hidden in the sealskin in order to make a cure for madness. I need that cure for the unicorn."

Nadin nodded. "But I'm still concerned about my lady. If she's a selkie, then Lord Watorej trapped her here."

"I know. I already figured that out. We can't do anything about that until the unicorn is cured." Adren fidgeted, restless at all this talk when they could be using the time to find what they needed. She started down the ladder.

"Yes we can. We can find both sealskins, give the lady hers, and get the other to the potion maker." Nadin stood at the top of the ladder, but didn't make a move to go down it.

"What if hers isn't in the mansion? If we cure the unicorn, it can help us find it and rescue her," said Adren as she motioned for him to follow. He didn't budge.

"We'll just have to keep on looking for it after we've found yours. I can't sit and wait for you and your unicorn if I can help her right now."

"And I can't wait if I can help the unicorn right now," Adren said, letting steel enter her voice.

"Lady Watorej has been held captive here for five years and

is being made to pretend she's human. No one's helped her. No one's even known she needed help. It's our duty to do all we can the moment we can." He sat down, arms crossed. Adren felt about ready to grab him by the shirt and drag him after her.

"The unicorn has been trapped by madness for as long as I can remember, maybe even longer. I am the only one who has ever cared enough to help it. I will not abandon it. Not ever."

Nadin shook his head. Never mind dragging him; Adren wanted to grab him by the shoulders and shake him to pieces. How could he not see? She would never abandon the lady. The unicorn came first, it always had, and once it was healed, she could come for the lady. Five years was long, true enough, and waiting would be hard, but the unicorn needed the help more than the lady did. Adren paced, trying to find a way to convince Nadin out of his stubbornness. There had to be something in his life that compared…

"If you had a cure for your mother, would you waste any time in giving it to her? After having worked so long, would you make her wait any more?" Nadin rubbed his nose, his expression softening. "I've put everything I've ever wanted in life aside to find a cure for the unicorn, and it has taken me years to get to this point. I won't let anything get in my way. The lady has to wait."

"Only if we at least try to find her sealskin while we're looking for yours," said Nadin, one of his knees starting to jiggle. Adren held back a smile.

"Fine. But we go once I have mine."

Nadin nodded and climbed down the ladder.

"Where to next?" he asked. Adren resisted the urge to shrug.

"Depends on what you see." Nadin stared at her, eyes wide. "Get going."

"I can't. I'll lose it again and then we won't be able to figure out anywhere to go. Please, just give me a starting point."

Excellent. Adren understood that his magic required him to be alert and relaxed, but she didn't have the time for this.

"No. Find it again."

"What if I can't?"

Ugh. Nadin really needed to work on this lack of self-confidence thing, no matter how common a problem it was for humans his age.

"Magic doesn't leave because you have difficulties using it. You either have it, or you don't. And you do." Nadin opened his mouth. "Don't argue. Find something." He closed his mouth and bit his lip, but he scanned the area.

"Right there," he said, pointing.

Not long after, Adren stared at the clock in the library.

"This?" she asked, jerking her thumb at it. Nadin nodded. "Then how do we open it?" He shrugged. Glaring at him, Adren ran her fingers along the sides of the clock's body, starting where she had left off earlier that day, but the only seam she could find was where pieces of wood had been joined. She stepped back.

"Maybe I'm wrong and it's in the next room," Nadin said, rubbing his neck.

"Or you're right and it's here, but needs magic to open it." Considering Lord Watorej's insistence that his possessions be cleaned as often as they were, Adren doubted he would have hid such a valuable item where servants could get at it when they needed to oil the gears. She made a noise of displeasure, at which Nadin gave a nervous glance.

"What kind of magic does it need?"

"I don't know. An enchantment of some kind. You're going to have to do it." When he and the unicorn had first met, he'd attacked it with magic, for which reason Adren was fairly certain he had raw magic. Which she didn't. Having him around had come in more handy than she had expected.

"You can't?"

"No, I just like to watch you sweat." She gave a wry look.

He made a face, then turned his attention to the clock, after which he made several more faces, each one more interesting than the last. When Adren was sure that the clock had him baffled, he touched it on the side and the front fell off, landing right on his feet. At which point he grimaced, bit his lip, and spent the next short while perfecting his impression of steam escaping from a kettle. Adren had to press her hand to her mouth to keep from laughing. She watched with amusement as he carefully removed his feet from underneath the wood and let it down such that it didn't make a noise once it touched the floor.

"There it is," he said, his voice strained.

Inside the clock body was an entire sealskin, whole as if the rest of the body had been sucked from it. It was folded awkwardly in order to fit inside, but Adren could see the head and flippers clearly. It also seemed the most ridiculous thing possible to hide a jewel in after they'd pulled it out and found it was as long as she was tall. She dragged it off the clock's front, which Nadin lifted and set back into place.

"This is heavier than I expected," Adren said.

"It's also hers."

No. No, no, no. "It can't be, or she'd have found it by now."

"Only if selkies can feel where their skins are..." Nadin paused and raised his index finger. "No, that wouldn't have helped her. The clock's enchantment drowns out the sealskin. And it's definitely hers. Its magic feels like her magic."

"Then where is the sealskin I need?" Adren asked, her gut clenched. But she knew where it was, even before Nadin said.

"Right here. I don't think that potion maker told you the whole truth. I mean, think! Why would anyone keep a sealskin without making it into clothing or something? Why would a potion maker, someone who knows about magic, want to have a sealskin in the first place? And what are the odds of both Lord Watorej and a potion maker wanting sealskins that have to do with magic while there's a selkie here in the mansion?"

Much as she had already acknowledged the possibility, Adren didn't like the feeling that the unicorn's cure had slipped, just a bit, from her fingers. Again. She wished she could get the jewel out, but remembered that the potion maker had said that only she could remove it. To make matters worse, since Adren didn't know the size of the jewel, she might not be able to feel for it and check if it was really inside.

"Fine. Suppose this is the same skin. I need that cure. Even if this is another dead end, I'm not giving up until I know for sure. You and I both want to free your lady. How can we get both? Can you get the lady to come by the potion maker's shop at some point tomorrow morning?"

"I can try." His tone was unconvincing.

"I need more than that. You have to get her near the shop or in the shop while she's acting like a human being, and it needs to be when I'm there giving the potion maker the sealskin so that we can see how the potion maker reacts. Once we see that, I'll be able to figure out why she said the sealskin was hers to begin with, and I'll be able to find a way for us to make happen everything we want to happen." She rolled up the sealskin.

"Isn't there a way to figure that out without having to do anything?" Nadin asked. Adren raised an eyebrow. "I mean, can't we just think about it and come to a conclusion that way?"

"If you want to make a plan based on assumptions and judgements, you go right ahead. I need solid information. Now help me get out of here."

Nadin shrugged and led the way.

Carrying the sealskin was awkward at first, and Nadin helped as they went down the stairs to the first floor but, after a few adjustments, Adren could soon manage. Or thought she could. They had nearly reached the garage when they a woman cried out, at first unintelligibly, then with two distinct words:

"My skin!"

Adren and Nadin exchanged a look of terror, and he would have broken into a run had she not shaken her head. If they ran, whoever had heard the lady would hear them and come after them as well. Instead, she walked as fast as possible and Nadin kept pace. Footsteps pounded above them as people woke and went after the lady. Nadin gestured at Adren to run, probably thinking they wouldn't be heard in the noise, but she shook her head again and glared for good measure. This close, they shouldn't take any chances.

The people upstairs must have found Lady Watorej, because they stopped running, and Adren could hear the lady shriek about her skin, the ocean, and covering her nakedness. It took everything Adren had in her not to run up the stairs and give the lady back her sealskin. This was for the unicorn.

But it still felt so wrong.

Nadin opened the door to the garage and let Adren in before he followed, checking the door after he closed it to make sure the inside had locked. Then he ran and grabbed a ring of keys, unlocked the outside door, and let Adren out. She peeked around the corner to make sure that none of Lord Watorej's security officers were nearby, then started on her way.

"Wait, Adren!" whispered Nadin. "When are you going to the potion maker's shop? And where is it, anyways? And how are you going to get in there without anyone seeing it if he discovers the sealskin's gone?"

"I'll be there the same time I met you about the plan, and it's on the east side of town, in that rough part, and invisibility, remember?" To keep the use of that to a minimum, she would have to circle around town, but she was sure she'd manage.

Nadin nodded, but he drew his eyebrows together.

"Be careful."

Adren hadn't heard that phrase spoken to her in years. It sounded odd. She cleared her throat, decided against talking, and returned the nod before heading away from the lord's property and towards her camp.

Tomorrow, the two of them would make this right.

Chapter Six

Adren shifted the weight of her pack again as she decided which way to take to the potion maker's shop. When she had woken earlier that morning and imagined keeping the sealskin invisible the entire way to the shop, she'd felt more than a little dread at the prospect. Even rolled up, it was annoying to carry around, especially as Adren preferred to have her hands free. Thank the saints her pack, once emptied, could carry and conceal the rolled-up skin. It had taken some work to hide all its contents around the camp, since the food had had to be hung from a tree to keep it out of reach of bears or other troublesome animals, but it made the journey much easier. She still opted for a roundabout route to the potion maker's shop, though, as she preferred not to deal with someone from the mansion recognizing her and asking why she wasn't over there. Otherwise, the livery, which she'd kept on, gave her an appearance of respectability. If needed, she could always pretend to be on an errand for Lord Watorej.

Most of the route went through the forest, so Adren took the opportunity to coax the unicorn to come with her. Its emotions had been fuzzy with an intrusion of its madness, but that meant it stayed closer to her out of paranoia. She didn't mind, though, and put her arm over its shoulders as they walked together.

Rain came in patches and the unicorn would shake its mane

when it stopped, spattering Adren with droplets. She'd been annoyed at the livery's lack of hood, but now, with a grin, she shook her head right back. The unicorn jumped in surprise, but its emotions cleared at her amusement and it returned the favour with the next pause in precipitation.

The corners of Adren's mouth turned down. When she had first realized there was something wrong with the unicorn, she had tried things like this, tried to play with it and encourage healing that way. But healing never came. And, much as she could calm it through control of her own feelings, Adren had no illusions about the fact that that amounted to nothing more than emotional manipulation. No matter how necessary it might be in the moment, Adren hated every time she had to use their connection to make the unicorn act how she wanted.

Something tickled her ear, so she turned to take in a rather lovely view of the unicorn's nostrils. It snorted, spraying bits of snot, its chuckle clear in Adren's mind. She raised an eyebrow.

"Was that really necessary?" She pushed its nose away, letting it prance a bit and enjoy its victory while she planned retaliation. Another patch of drizzle had started, so Adren cupped her hands. When the unicorn returned to her side, she threw the water at its neck, but some of it escaped her control and splashed into the unicorn's eye.

This, of course, meant war. The unicorn shook every part of itself it could, coming closer and closer to Adren as she raised her hands to defend herself from the onslaught. She laughed and tried to back away just as the unicorn pushed her with its nose and, caught off balance, she toppled. Its head in her face again, the unicorn blew on her. Adren gave a long, full-on belly laugh and, before she pushed it out of her way, hugged its neck and gave it a kiss below the horn.

Would the unicorn joke around like this when it was well? Adren had not met any others. Still, mad as it was, Adren could see traces of the true nature and power of a unicorn in it, which gave her faith that not all was lost. Its pranks may be part of its insanity but, if all that insanity had done was cover up, hide the unicorn's beauty, then nothing in the world could convince Adren that her search was in vain.

When the time came to enter the town, Adren and the unicorn parted ways again. The sun had come out by this point, hot and bright, to dry the world, and Adren made her way to the potion maker's shop. A customer had the potion maker's full attention, so Adren pretended to inspect the bottles on display. They were full of various kinds and colours of liquid—and some filled with what was most definitely not liquid—with several oddly warm to the touch and all unidentifiable. Of course, they had neat labels, which she scrutinized as she had seen others do when they were indecisive. Could everyone here read, or did the illiterate ones just hide it well?

The customer left after thanking the potion maker far more than Adren thought decent, and the potion maker flipped the sign on the door before approaching Adren.

"Ah, a potion for strength or a treatment for boils. Such a difficult choice," the potion maker observed in a dry tone. Adren put down the bottles a little more firmly than she'd intended. She turned and attempted a smile. The potion maker eyed the pack. "Did you really manage to get it?"

"Of course I did," said Adren, and she took off the pack and emptied it to prove her words.

At first, when the potion maker saw the sealskin, she didn't seem to recognize it but, once it was unrolled, she bit her lip.

"I hadn't expected that you would really be able to steal it. It looks like you've defied expectation again."

"Again?" Adren clenched her fists, her tone steely. The potion maker at least had the decency to look embarrassed.

"I don't like telling any potential customers, especially determined and capable ones such as yourself, that I can't give them what they want... so I try to deter them in other ways."

"You can't make the cure." It didn't matter how many times this moment had come, each time made Adren want to scream, want to grab the person in front of her and shake them and shake them and shake them until the world changed and the unicorn didn't need her anymore. But this time she had the voice of a selkie in her ears, screaming for her skin as Adren stole it. If Adren normally got frosty with her anger, now she was glacial.

"No, I can't." The potion maker hung her head.

Adren considered tearing the woman limb from limb. Instead, acutely aware of the unicorn's emotions, she stuffed her anger back down into her heart as she rolled the sealskin up again to put it back into her pack.

"Don't—"

"What?"

The potion maker shrank back at Adren's gaze. "I was hoping to keep that, now that it's here." The gall of the woman!

"Oh, certainly."

"Really?"

"When the hell-gods decide to give mercy."

The shop door opened and Adren closed her pack to hide the sealskin. The potion maker turned to the new customers and froze, mouth half open. Adren shouldered the pack and raised her head only to find that Nadin and Lady Watorej had arrived.

"We saw the sign," said Nadin, his eyes flicking towards Adren, "but I promised my lady that you'd have something to help her sleep. She's been having nightmares, and the doctors' remedies haven't helped." The lady nodded, her gaze clear and actions crisp. Adren could offer a guess or two as to what those nightmares might be.

"He assured me you would have something, and I am so anxious to sleep more comfortably that I insisted we come in. The intrusion is entirely my fault."

"It is no intrusion, my Lady Watorej," said the potion maker with a bow. "I have several potions for sleeping problems, here in the corner. Please, survey them and see if there is one that addresses your ailment. I will only be a few moments with this customer and then I will be able to help you."

"Thank you."

Adren watched the potion maker as the lady and Nadin passed, waiting for some betrayal of her true emotions. She expected anger, perhaps greed if all the potion maker hoped for from the lady was money. What she saw was very different. As the two passed, the potion maker's gaze went between the lady and Adren, so briefly that Adren almost didn't catch it, accompanied by an expression of calculated anticipation.

So, the potion maker knew the lady was a selkie, but how did she plan to exploit this knowledge? What could she hope to gain that Lord Watorej's pursuit wouldn't jeopardize?

"I want to keep it," said the potion maker to Adren in a low voice. "I know what to do with it. You'll likely just sell it and be done with it. If it's money you want, I can pay you. What do you think of three thousand keb?"

With that money, one could fill Nadin's livery barn with horses and tack. It was a desperate price, but only to anyone who didn't know how much money Adren had left behind the last time she'd been in this shop. Three thousand keb lost from that would still leave the potion maker with more money than she'd likely ever had at one time. The best way to tell how much someone needed an object was to find out not how much they were willing to pay, but how much of what they had they were willing to give up.

"Six hundred olen." Twenty four thousand keb. A fifth more than what Adren had stolen for the potion maker.

"Agreed."

All the saints and gods besides, that easily? Adren resisted the urge to look at the lady. The last thing she needed right now was to give away what she knew.

"I never expected you would agree to pay so much; that's why I asked for it. It's not for sale." Oh, did it feel good to say that, but not so good that Adren missed the flash of pure fury on the potion maker's face at those words. It gave Adren pause. In all the years of her search, she had never seen someone so angry when their wishes had been thwarted. There was something deeper here than simple greed. She and Nadin had to free the lady, then she and the unicorn had to get out of town, before the potion maker chose to act on her wrath.

Adren left the shop without another word. Once outside, she ducked into an alley to wait for Nadin and the lady to follow. They did so in only a few moments. As they went back along the winding street, Adren stepped out of the alley and was about to join them when the potion maker appeared at the door of her shop, staring out after the lady. The potion maker saw Adren and raised her eyebrows. Then she, one side of her mouth lifted, she turned back and pointed all the fingers of one hand at the lady.

She was about to perform a spell and the lady wouldn't be able to stand it. It was like a punch in the gut to Adren. Those fingers tensed. Adren ran out between the potion maker and the lady, just in time for the spell to slam into her with the brunt of its power. The magic ripped through her like lightning, slipped down her arms and legs, rooted her to the spot. She could tell that this spell, once complete, would give the potion maker control over Adren's will and body.

Everything within her that could fight it, did, but that only caused her more pain. She tried to scream, but nothing would come. The unicorn's eagerness to protect sang through her but, when she tried to calm herself, the spell furthered its attack. So she tried to bolster her resistance again, only to intensify her emotions. Only to intensify the burning. She could not do both. She had to, but the balance could not be kept; she could not have victory with both.

The blackened, fogged portion of her mind throbbed within her, as if its experience of her pain came as the empathy of a separate being. Its activity unnerved her, but it was the only part of her that the magic had not yet touched. Already, the spell had subdued every other part of her, and now it closed in on that place that she never even peered into for too long. She could see the encounter in her mind, the black part encased in thick glass and the magic as tendrils of shivering light reaching out to touch it. At first, they simply felt its resistance, but then they charged at it and the glass cracked. Again, they bashed themselves against the barrier and the crack widened, opening a small sliver.

And something came out.

Another magic rushed through the crack, enraged. It poured like a flood over the spell, its waters overwhelming the feeble tentacles, washing them away as it filled her entire being. No, not like water. Like lightning. Like fire. But the kind that burned without consuming. Adren regained her power of movement in a moment and leapt towards the potion maker, knife out. The woman tried to flee, but Adren grabbed her and put the weapon to her throat. She wasn't about to let the woman get anywhere near the lady and Nadin.

"Promise me you will never use that spell again," Adren said, blade pressed against the potion maker's skin.

"I promise," she said, trembling.

"Now, we're going to go inside and you're going to give me back every single bit of my money." Adren wanted to interrogate the woman, but Nadin and the lady were getting farther away with every breath. Once all five hundred olen were stowed in Adren's coat, she put the knife away and knocked the potion maker out the same way she had Nadin when they'd met in the garage. She ran in the direction Nadin and the lady had gone, hoping to catch them before they reached the mansion.

The only problem was that, no matter how far she went, she couldn't find them. They had to have taken a turn at some point, but where? The unicorn's fright for her, still not abated from the encounter with the spell, only grew as it began its approach. Adren tried to calm herself, but the potion maker should have returned to consciousness and could be coming after either Adren or the lady. Not to mention this new magic pumping through her veins, soaking into every part of her body. Adren didn't believe for a moment the potion maker had told the truth when she promised not to use that spell again. While she'd be a fool to use it again on Adren, she'd most definitely use it on anyone else who came in her way. And, now that she'd shown her hand and it hadn't succeeded, she'd be scared. She wouldn't be acting rationally. Adren needed to get ahead of her. Now.

Gods in hell, but these roads were infuriating! No matter which she picked, they always led her the wrong way, which made it difficult for the unicorn to come to her, but provided no other benefit. The magic pulsed within her, begged to be used, but she dared not touch it. Without any skill with it, even the skill a child who had grown up with it would have, anything could happen. And not a good anything. Oh but, sweet saints, it was tempting. It felt like… like living song. Like what the sun would sound like if all its being were turned into music, or if the ocean were given a voice instead of wordless roaring. Adren had never experienced its like before and, while she knew she should fear it, all it brought was peace.

She shook her head to clear it of such thoughts. She couldn't give in to them. The magic hadn't even finished filling her yet. It may come to the point where she could afford to ignore it no longer, but for now she would.

Ah! There! The dye shop of the annoying woman with the bangles. This wasn't the direction Adren had thought she was going, but no matter. She could head to the mansion by way of Nadin's house and hope to all the saints that Nadin had enough sense not to have taken a direct route back. Still, Nadin would be returning home after this errand, so she could find him, at least. Part human as he was, she hoped his fairy ancestry was enough to ensure she could depend on his help.

When she reached Nadin's house, she broke into a run, pushing past those who were too slow to get out of her way. Someone came by on a horse and they nearly collided, but she swerved at the last instant. The horse spooked and broke into a gallop, leaving the rider to swear at it for as long as Adren could hear his voice and the pounding of hooves. She paid it no mind. All her attention focused on the mansion. The sooner she arrived, the sooner she could leave the town and lead everyone to safety.

At first, she couldn't see Lady Watorej or Nadin, so she had to force herself to slow. Even so, it wasn't until Adren was only a few steps away from the grounds that she saw them. They had just turned onto the street. She ran to them.

"You're in danger," Adren told the lady.

"From who?" The lady put a hand to her chest.

"Is it—?" Nadin started, and Adren nodded.

"The potion maker knows what you are and she will use you if we don't leave town."

"I'm afraid I have no idea what you're talking about."

Honeysuckle spread across Adren's mouth, the taste so amplified by the magic that it hurt. If it hadn't have been for Nadin seeing both the lady and the sealskin as having the same magic, Adren would have believed her. It looked as though she had been right: her sense picked up not so much on truth as what someone was convinced in both mind and heart was true. Lord Watorej would have a lot to answer for when the time came for the consequences of his actions to catch up to him.

"You may not understand, my lady," Nadin said, "but you have to trust her."

"Why doesn't my husband know about this?"

"He does." The lie burned on her tongue as strongly as the truth had sweetened it. "He asked Nadin and myself to keep you safe, once we knew for sure where the danger was coming from." The inside of her mouth ached, but she kept from betraying it. They couldn't afford the time that would be lost explaining the true situation. Lady Watorej pressed her lips together.

"My lady, you know my reputation. Trust us," said Nadin.

The lady paused. "Then what do we need to do?" They both looked at Adren.

"We need to get out of town, now. Once we're out, we can make a plan, but we need to go before the potion maker comes to take you."

"Lead on, then."

Adren took a deep breath, then headed towards the edge of the town. It was the quickest route not only away from the lord, but also towards where it was safe for the unicorn whenever it arrived. Something seemed to have confused it, and it wasn't taking as straight a route to her as it normally would.

Despite both of them being taller than her, the lady and Nadin could not keep up with Adren's pace and they had to stop to catch their breath more than Adren liked. Once they were in the forest, she allowed them to slow, but she found it odd she could go so much longer and faster than they. Her stamina was great in general, but it seemed to have increased since earlier that day. How deeply had this new magic affected her?

Lady Watorej and Nadin were both flushed and panting by the time they reached Adren's camp. While they caught their breath, Adren leaned against a tree, clenching her fists to keep from shaking. The sounds of the forest soothed her—robins singing, the wind in the trees—and the dappled light through needled branches brought with it a warmth that the light breeze didn't negate, but softened with coolness.

It felt healing, this balance. Everything fit and had order, an order that brought beauty with it. The countryside had always suited Adren better than human communities, but the woods held a special peace for her. She didn't think much about what she hoped for herself after the unicorn was cured except when she would stand under the trees and stare at the sky. However long this took her, however far, wherever she ended up, there had to be a forest. As that dream rose within her again, she was able to relax. The unicorn, soothed, finally stopped its approach. Thank the saints.

Now, the lady.

She and Nadin had sat down, Nadin right on top of where Adren had hidden some of her supplies. He'd caught the corner of a pot without knowing it and kept making unsuccessful attempts to get comfortable. Adren decided not to tell him. His squirms were entertaining.

The lady's condition, on the other hand, was not. It could be that Lord Watorej had placed a spell on her or hired someone to do so, causing her to forget her true self. If this were so, then they had little hope of recovering her, and Adren prayed this wasn't. Considering the actions of the potion maker and what Nadin said about the sealskin's and the lady's magic being one and the same, Adren now doubted the sealskin contained a jewel, magic or otherwise, which meant that she had no tool to combat any tampering with the lady's mind. But, if the jewel didn't exist, then that meant Lord Watorej hadn't had a tool to tamper with her mind, so… she took off her pack and pulled out the sealskin.

"Nadin, do you remember that first magical thing you found in the mansion and then lost track of?"

"Yes."

"What was it?"

Nadin swallowed, then looked at the lady. Adren couldn't tell if this was a signal or if he was reluctant to talk about his magic in front of Lady Watorej. She raised her eyebrows and inclined her head. His response was to pretend to scratch his face while pointing with that hand in the lady's direction. The lady followed this interaction with interest and, even though Nadin froze when she turned her attention to him, smiled as if she'd just figured out the rules to a secret game.

"You two think I have some kind of magic in me," she said.

"Not think," Adren said. "Know." She spread the sealskin out in front of the lady. If anything would remind a selkie of their true nature, it was their skin. The lady opened her mouth as if to speak, frowned, closed it. Her hands began to tremble and she clasped them together, holding them close to her body. Good. It was working.

"I know—" But her mouth snapped shut before she could finish her sentence. All she seemed to be able to do was stare and stare and stare, caught by the magic of the sealskin. Caught by her magic. One of her hands freed itself from the grasp of the other as she reached out, her fingers stretching, stretching, stretching until she could almost touch it—

"My lady."

She pulled her hand back as if she had been burned, and Adren glared at Nadin. He shook his head at her.

"I know what that is," said the lady, her tongue loosed from whatever had made her keep it still.

"Then you know that using it now wouldn't be a good idea," Nadin said. Adren realized he had been wiser than she. If the lady had touched the skin, enraptured as she had been, she would have used it to transform, and it was best to hold off until they'd found the ocean. A seal was not fit for the forest.

"Aye, 'tis so." The lady sighed, her gaze wistful. She drew her knees to her chest and wrapped her arms around her legs. "And it will never be mine again." It broke Adren's heart. She wanted to explain everything, especially the part where she and Nadin didn't really work for Lord Watorej.

And she would have, too, if the unicorn's fear had not entered her, a black blade that shot through their connection. She became stiff, and Nadin raised a hand to her, but she couldn't respond. The fear opened like a deadly flower, shifting to unbridled terror in an instant and growing with such speed that she had to use all her power to keep it from overwhelming her.

Then the potion maker's spell struck the unicorn. Adren could feel it working, a pain that the magic within her only heightened. The unicorn fought the spell, and the backlash tore through both it and Adren, causing her to double over.

"Not again, not again, not again..." Adren couldn't stop saying it or else she was sure the pain would overwhelm her. "Not again, not again, not again, not again..." Her face became a mask of agony, frozen in its distortion and she could not relax it. Spell-magic attacked the unicorn, attacked the back of Adren's mind, like the lightning of a thousand storms all striking the same place at the same time. The unicorn had lost control of its body and was rapidly losing control of its mind. It needed her help, but Adren could do nothing. Even if it had been right next to her, this secondhand experience held such strength that it had incapacitated her completely.

Oh, saints, the spell had found the link between the unicorn and Adren. That was the last of the unicorn that remained out of its control. It poised, that hateful tendril of magic, as if posturing for an audience, then struck. It wrapped itself around the link and clogged it. The unicorn vanished from Adren's mind. All she could feel there now was a throbbing where the spell had coiled itself. It was so small.

The release left Adren gasping as if she'd been underwater the whole time and only now had a chance to breathe. She found herself staring at her knees. She straightened, still trying to get her breathing under control, and suffered an immediate attack of vertigo.

"Adren, what happened?" asked Nadin, now standing himself. So dizzy she was about to fall over, Adren closed her eyes and gestured at him to wait. Once the vertigo had passed, she could speak again.

"The potion maker put the unicorn under a spell." Adren ignored the lady's confused expression and focused on Nadin.

"You felt that? How?"

"Never mind how! She found it and she's controlling it. We need to do something." The back of her mind felt so empty; as if her thoughts echoed across a vacant theatre. She resisted   the urge to curl up and bury her head in her arms.

"How did she find it? How did she even know about it? Where did she get the ability to do that kind of thing?" Nadin had chosen the worst time to be this thick.

"Never mind *how* it happened," Adren bit off every word short, her jaw clenched in anger. "The unicorn needs our help." The grief within her touched the edge of the place where the unicorn had been, at first constrained by long habit but then, finding no resistance, it flooded through Adren, larger than she had thought it could be. Tears formed in her eyes and her inability to do much more than slow them made her angry.

Nadin opened his mouth, but the lady put a hand on his shoulder. For a long, silent moment, Adren struggled to regain some semblance of order within herself.

"Where is the unicorn? What need we do to help it?" asked the lady, her voice gentle.

"I don't know," Adren whispered. A tear slipped through her control and ran down her cheek, past her mouth to her chin. It pooled, too small even to drip. "I can't feel it anymore."

Chapter Seven

The place where the unicorn's emotions used to reside felt like the spot where... Adren lost her grip on the memory and it tumbled into the dark place in her mind. There were too many places, too many things taking up residence inside her. She wondered if she had ever—*could* ever—only be herself in her own body. The unicorn may have been gone, but the spell still pulsed in a tight knot that Adren couldn't reach; the dark place was as dark as ever and now there was this magic that slid inside her as if she'd been made to hold it. The fact that it had always been in her, hidden in that dark, fogged place, made her approach it a moment, curious about what else lay underneath before she recoiled. This new magic was trouble enough. The unicorn's plight was enough. The last thing Adren needed was to release anything else. Not that she was sure she could.

Around them, the trees dropped needles as a breeze passed through, high enough so Adren could feel little of its movement. The sun had reached its zenith, but clouds hung thick in the sky, having filled it in fits and starts since the rain that morning. Even the air felt thicker, closer, a weight that pressed itself against Adren's skin. The swaying of trees seemed a roar in her ears, the sun blinding when it broke through. This should not be happening here! Adren inhaled to steady herself, expecting to smell dirt, trees, and the freshness of leaves from the dogwood. All that came to her aid, plus, when the wind was at its height, the scent of seawater. The ocean. Finally, something she could use. She smiled.

"Do you know the way to the ocean from here?" she asked Lady Watorej. The lady nodded and pointed towards the source of the wind.

"'Tis but an inlet, and a small one for, but it is the ocean nonetheless. Why—?"

Adren waved a hand, both at the lady and her own worry. It only worked with the lady. Since the spell had found the connection between Adren and the unicorn, Adren was sure the potion maker would want to trade for the sealskin. Rare as the ingredients were that a unicorn carcass would supply, rare as the free use of the power a unicorn's horn was to a human, Adren knew how much the potion maker wanted the sealskin and the lady. But that was small consolation. Even if the potion maker didn't kill the unicorn or maim it in some way, she now knew how much it meant to Adren. There was no way of knowing how cruelly she would treat the unicorn if Adren didn't give her what she wanted. With that spell, the trauma inflicted would be far more insidious than the physical kind.

"We lied when we said we were working for Lord Watorej," Adren said. Blood pounded in her ears. "We're here to free you from him and the potion maker, but now the potion maker has something precious to me, so you need to tell me everything you know about the two of them and why the potion maker wants you so badly."

"Adren!" Nadin was aghast. "Don't you know how to speak to nobility properly?"

The lady laughed. "Oh, I am no true noble, only taken in marriage by one." Nadin sat back, only somewhat mollified. "It may not give much help, but I will tell you what I know."

"Anything more than I already know would be a help."

"I dearly hope that is so. But where to start?" The lady tapped her chin. "Yes. It's always the beginning that's best, isn't it? It happened like this: before he took me, five years past, my family and I would come to the inlet and become human to rest and feel the sand between our toes. Lord Watorej watched us. He thought we knew naught of him, but he hides poorly. So, we set a guard of two on our skins, lest he take one. After a time, he would try to speak with me when I was with only one or two of my family. I liked him then. He caused no harm and seemed to have no intent for such. As our friendship grew, it was clear he wanted more and, though I also desired it, I could see no future for us. What human here would accept our union? What could he give that would satisfy the loss of the sea? But he saw it not so and went to the potion maker for help.

"One day, while I and my brother guarded the skins, a spell fell over me. I fought it with my magic, but in vain, and lost myself. I could do nothing while the potion maker, who had cast the spell, bid me take my skin and run to her while Lord Watorej fought my brother and kept him from me. We then left that place such that none of my family could follow, and he hid from me my skin. And so, even with the spell gone from me, I could do naught but what he wished, for I could not escape him. I had been losing myself in pieces ever since, but whether that is from the doctor's treatment or the separation from my skin, I cannot say."

"That doesn't explain why she wants you or your skin." Adren pressed her chin into one hand and rested the elbow the other. "She was willing to pay over five hundred olen for it."

"Five hundred olen? How would she even get that kind of money?" asked Nadin. Adren raised an eyebrow. "You mean you…" He turned pale.

"I got it back," Adren replied, irritated.

"Will you return it to Lord Watorej?"

"Maybe."

"Um."

"Don't faint on me, now."

Nadin's face had approached Adren's natural skin colour. He sat down.

"I recall something more," said the lady, "of the potion

maker. After Lord Watorej had my skin, they two argued. I was too frightened to hear all, but it seemed mayhap that they had an agreement of some kind, and that he had broken it. 'Twas to do with me in some way... he had promised her my help, perhaps? But he was not true to his word, and she was angry for it. I was glad—she has terrifying power."

As the lady mentioned this, the part of the spell in Adren's mind jiggled, then widened to open a slight gap. Adren lifted her head and turned all her attention to that single point within her, trying not to hope too greatly. A trickle of emotion came through from the unicorn, but it was fuzzy, as if the unicorn were asleep. Oh, thank the saints! She stood.

"What is it?" asked Nadin.

"I can find the unicorn again." Adren rolled up the sealskin and opened her pack.

"You can't take that with you," said Nadin. "That's exactly what she wants!"

"Which is why we're taking it." She shoved the skin into her pack, which she then handed to Nadin. He shook his head.

"I'm staying here with Lady Watorej. Lord Watorej has to be looking for her now, and we can't leave her by herself."

Adren rolled her eyes. "I'm not leaving her." Then she addressed the lady. "If the potion maker really wants you and your skin, we'll have to convince her we're willing to give it and you to her before we can free the unicorn." The lady nodded.

"I would not wish to bring thee more sorrow than thou hast already endured. But, please, let me carry what is mine." She reached for the pack.

"I'm not like you," said Adren, stunned by the lady's use of thou, but she gave her what she wanted.

"We can't do this without a plan!" Nadin's colour had returned and he rose to his feet. "My lady, if you come, you'll be putting yourself in danger. She could put that spell of hers on you again, and then we'd have saved you from one person only for you to be captured by someone else. I can't let that happen to you! We have to take you to the ocean so you can escape. We'll get the unicorn back some other way." Nadin's voice shook with anger of an intensity that surprised Adren. He hadn't even been this passionate when he told her about his mother.

"And what if the potion maker kills the unicorn as a result?" she pointed out. "She could get a lot of money from the horn, never mind the internal organs, blood, bones, and hide. Believe me, I know what kinds of things people do at a chance like this."

"She might not be after money."

"All humans are after money."

"I'm not."

Sweet saints. Not *now*.

"I won't sit here talking any longer while I could be doing," Adren said through gritted teeth.

"We can't be doing if we don't know what we're doing," Nadin shot back.

"We *do* know. We're going after the unicorn."

"And then what?"

"We decide as we walk," said the lady, who had put her hands between the two of them.

Nadin flushed and mumbled, "I hadn't thought of that."

Adren spun on her heel and headed off, the lady beside her. Nadin, caught by surprise, had to jog to catch up to them.

The fact that Nadin kept trying to make a plan didn't sway Adren in the least. The mansion may have been Nadin's terrain, but this was Adren's. And the potion maker's, in a sense. No detailed plot would work here and the sooner he learned that, the better. Even if someone came up with what seemed the perfect strategy, there were always variables no one could predict. Reality would tear to pieces any person who thought they could succeed by way of a complicated plan, flexible as it may be. Adren knew this only too well.

As soon as they had neared the unicorn, she left them with the excuse of seeking information. She would have told the lady what she was about to do, but not Nadin. Something about his defense of humans had got under her skin, and it rankled. Her original assessment of his nature had been only a guess after all. It was an educated one, but a guess nonetheless. Which hadn't bothered her too much, except for the doubt that now stepped out of the shadows to be examined. She had trusted him so far, and he hadn't broken that trust, but that may only be for so long. If only she had some kind of proof of his character. But she couldn't obtain it, not yet. When she came close enough to the unicorn, she turned herself invisible and crept forward.

Both unicorn and potion maker stood in a clearing by the inlet. The potion maker had her head tilted to one side, and her eyes didn't seem to focus on her surroundings. If anything, she was listening.

"Hiding won't do you any good," said the woman. "The unicorn can feel that you're here." That dratted spell. Adren should have expected this.

Since the less the potion maker knew about Adren's magic the better, she stepped back into a hiding place where she let herself become visible again. With only hours of experience with the connection, the potion maker wouldn't be able to tell changes in distance to the degree of accuracy that Adren could. Even Adren herself couldn't give anything beyond rough estimates, despite years of practise. As her chest relaxed, Adren walked out to the potion maker.

The unicorn stood, dull-eyed, and so, so still. Not a twitch. Not even a sound.

"Where is the sealskin?" asked the potion maker.

"Nearby."

"And the selkie?"

"Also nearby."

"Why aren't they here?" The potion maker squinted and searched the trees behind Adren.

"I didn't know this was a trade."

"What else would it be? I have something you care about, and you have what I want. If you give them to me, I'll take the spell off the unicorn."

"And let it go without causing it further harm," Adren said, her tone final. She had no intention of giving the potion maker a loophole. Even if the woman backed out on her promise, Adren wasn't about to be stupid and let her.

"For the selkie, I will let the unicorn go. For the skin, I will remove the spell. Do this promptly, and I will cause the unicorn no further harm."

This wording Adren found interesting. As far as she had understood, removing the spell was the same as letting the unicorn go. Either the potion maker had a piece in play that had yet to be revealed, or she was bluffing, or she'd made an honest mistake with her wording. Adren doubted the latter, but couldn't tell which one of the others was accurate. Considering her previous dealings with the potion maker, though, she felt safe enough taking a calculated risk to find out.

"I'll return soon." If she was going to talk to the lady alone, she would need to distract Nadin.

When she came to him and the lady, he asked her what she had discovered, but she didn't answer.

"I have an idea, but I need you to go that way"—she pointed away from where the unicorn and potion maker were—"to find the inlet. I'll stay with the lady." He nodded and headed out.

"Is the unicorn unharmed?" asked the lady.

"It is under the spell, and so is harmed, but no more shall come to pass." Adren slipped into the dialect more easily than she had expected, considering how long it had been since she had last used it in a real conversation. The two-sided kind. "What magic have you, besides that of transformation?"

"I am poor in the use of magic. Thou wilt find no weapon in me." The lady glanced where Nadin had gone. "Am I right in thinking that thou desirest him not in thy plan?"

"Call me not thou, an you please. I am not your kind." Adren gathered her thoughts. "He must needs be away for the plan I have begun. The potion maker shall release the unicorn from the spell for the sealskin. Have you any magic that might cause the unicorn to flee while I secure the skin?"

The lady shook her head. "Methinks you need Nadin. I would only become captive again."

"Nay, I need him not!"

"He hath helped you greatly. You would ignore all that?"

"It is because of what happens now that I trust him not. See you not yet how dishonest humans are? How they look only to their own gain?"

"Like you?"

"I am not like them."

"Nor are you like me. What are you then, an you are neither human nor magical creature? What then are you, an you fit not with the world as you perceive it?"

"I am myself. Now, aid me."

The lady shook her head. "Take the sealskin, an you wish, and enact your plan without me, or wait for him to return," She crossed her arms.

"You are adamant in this?"

"Aye."

"You will let me have your skin, with the trust that I can succeed alone?"

"Aye," said the lady, but after a pause. Before Adren could jump on that, the lady removed the pack and handed it over. "Take it and go. Methinks Nadin will return soon."

Adren took the pack and left. Saints. She had assumed the lady would understand and come to help a fellow magical creature, not that she would trust humans first. After all, all any human had done to her was imprison her and make her forget what and who she really was.

No matter. Adren would be able to free the unicorn, just as she would be able to find a cure. It might take a long time, and there might be several dead ends along the way, but it would come out in their favour. There was no other way to see it. None that she would agree to, anyways.

When Adren returned to the potion maker and the unicorn, she took out the sealskin at once for the potion maker to see.

"Now take off the spell. Or I won't bring you the selkie."

"Hand me the skin." Adren obeyed, ready to make the unicorn run. The potion maker set the sealskin on the ground before reaching into a pocket and pointing at the unicorn with all the fingers of the other. The coil of spell at the back of Adren's mind dissolved and all that remained were the unicorn's fuzzy emotions. Adren waited for more to happen, only to realize after the potion maker had lowered her hand that the unicorn was asleep. The eerie stillness had gone, replaced by closed eyes, soft breathing, and one hind leg lifted slightly off the ground. It wouldn't respond to her. Not in this state.

The potion maker chuckled. "My sleeping potions are just as effective on unicorns as they are on humans. I'll wake it up as soon as I have everything I asked for safely in my power. Otherwise, it won't wake until nightfall, and you don't want to wait until then."

Adren wasn't fazed. She may not be able to remove the unicorn from the situation, but she *could* remove the potion maker. The only question was how to do it without giving the potion maker enough time to put her spell on the unicorn again and tell it to attack. Adren knew without question that that was not a scenario she would survive.

She had her knife, but no skill in throwing it. And magic. It hummed, eager to act.

No, she dared not. She would not be able to bear it if she missed and hit the unicorn.

"I made it clear you wouldn't get the unicorn back without both the selkie and her skin in my possession. Did you think you could trick me?"

Yes.

"How did you learn about the unicorn?"

"I found your connection to it when I put the spell on you." The potion maker gave a crooked smile, her words confident save for a moment, a glimpse of wide eyes and stretched lips when the word "spell" left her mouth. Her next words came out in a rush: "Now go get the selkie, if you really have her here."

"And why do you think I, the one person you can't control, am also the one negotiating with you at this moment?"

"I don't follow."

"Lord Watorej is no fool. He will allow you to keep the sealskin, but he has no intention of giving you his wife." Adren didn't break eye contact with the potion maker, didn't move a muscle of her face despite the discomfort on her tongue. She knew the tells for a lie. The potion maker didn't. She paled, as Adren had hoped, but lifted her chin.

"So he will finally hold to that part of the bargain?"

"Yes."

The potion maker raised her eyebrows. "I find it interesting he would share the details of his deepest shame with a hireling. Or anyone, really."

"I am not just anyone."

"No, you're not. I've heard about you. They call you the White Changeling, don't they? Those you've worked with. You lie, you steal—don't think I don't know where you got that money from—you show no regard for human life, and for what? There are some who say you can't help yourself and search for a cure for your own madness. There are others who would rather just have you dead. So, suppose you tricked me, suppose you got away from this through foul play: how do you think those people would react when they knew the truth? How long do you think you and the unicorn would have?"

Adren's hands shook. She hadn't known there were people who hated her enough to want to kill her. And she didn't like that the potion maker had used that fact to control the conversation. "Why do you want the selkie?"

"Before the saints threw their creators into hell, people worshipped the gods. Some never stopped."

"That in no way answers my question."

"It wasn't meant to. You know, if you let me have the selkie, through her help I would become able to cure your unicorn."

After lying the exact same way twice, she thought she could fool Adren again? "Somehow, I doubt that."

"Well, I offered. Now." The potion maker raised her arm. "Will you give me what I want, or is it time to find a buyer for this carcass?" Her fingers, stiff, pointed at the unicorn.

Chapter Eight

Before Adren had a chance to respond, the potion maker's hand flew back and she cried out. Nadin ran up beside Adren.

"The lady told me where you were," he said, as if apologizing. "I found the inlet. Except it looks like you did, too..." She ignored him and leapt at the potion maker, who cradled her burnt hand. The woman's reactions were slow and she didn't defend herself until Adren had already reached into the potion maker's pocket and flung away the object she'd used in making the spell.

Still, the potion maker was wild. They grappled for longer than Adren had thought older woman would have stamina. Every time Adren would reach for her knife, the potion maker would block with one arm and swipe with the other. Adren grabbed both her wrists and held. The woman struggled, but kept pushing against the fingers—the strongest part of Adren's grip. Adren waited, letting the potion maker tire herself out. Then, as the potion maker lifted a foot to kick, Adren pushed with all her might until they had both fallen to the ground. Adren punched her across the jaw and she went limp.

"Do you still need—?"

"Go get the lady," Adren told Nadin and, as he ran off, she searched the potion maker's pockets for something, anything that would wake the unicorn. Unlike from the choke, recovery time from a punch was variable, and Adren couldn't afford to rely on events lining up in her favour. Saints knew they hadn't done so the entire time she'd been in this town.

The pockets were empty. Gods in hell, the potion maker must have planned to wake the unicorn using that object. And Adren had thrown it away.

For the next few moments, the forest was treated to such a colourful and inventive stream of cursing that even sailors might feel the need to cover their ears. When she had finished, Adren went to the unicorn, wishing she could shake it awake but, without a potion or magic to help, the unicorn slept too deeply for that. She put a hand on its shoulder, examined its wounds instead. They had closed over and, though there remained some swelling, none was in danger of opening up. Adren became grim at the thought of the opportunity this presented. Her hand hovered over the unicorn's flank.

Saints, she couldn't hesitate! The potion maker could wake at any minute. Eyes closed, Adren pressed into those red lines on the unicorn's flank. Never had she thought she would need to cause the unicorn this kind of pain. Especially not to free it from sleep. Its muscles twitched, but its mind didn't clear. She kept pressing, harder, as hard as she dared before her stomach knotted and she had to keep from retching.

"Adren!" It was Nadin's voice, at a full shout. With a glance back to make sure the potion maker was still unconscious, Adren looked for him, but could see neither him nor the lady. "Lord Watorej!" he yelled, and his voice cracked. Adren's heart skipped a beat. Of course he'd find them now, of all times. He would come in and ruin everything before she could finish with the potion maker. Idiot humans.

There was a bang and horses screaming, followed by the smell of ash. Nadin must have used magic to defend the lady. Adren hoped he wasn't stupid enough to let anyone see him do it, if he wanted to keep his job and care for his mother.

The lady ran through the trees, nearly tripping in her haste.

"Get me my skin!" Adren obeyed at once. Lady Watorej took it, went into the inlet, and looked back.

Six people on horseback entered the clearing. Adren drew her knife and adopted a fighting stance, watching the four officers that came behind on foot, two of them holding Nadin. They and the riders formed a ring around Adren and the lady, saltwater splashing the legs and flanks of those horses that entered the inlet. At first, Adren thought the lord hadn't joined the search, but one rider came forward and she recognized him. Lord Watorej. The way his attention went straight to the lady to the exclusion of all else sent shivers down Adren's spine.

"Come home," he said to her, his voice surprisingly gentle. "You aren't well."

"Nay, my lord, not I."

"Please, allow the doctor to see to you. If you would come—" He reached out a hand, but the lady pulled back.

"*You* are a child who thinks love means all must sacrifice at his altar. I will have no more of it." Then, with a mouthed "thank you" to Adren, the lady pressed the sealskin to her body and dove. As Lord Watorej dismounted and drew his sword, a seal's tail disappeared into the water. His body swayed as if in the crossroad of two conflicting paths: one drew him into the ocean, the other rooted him to the shore.

The shore won; he spun on his heel and surveyed the scene. His eyes widened when he saw the unicorn, then widened even more when he saw the potion maker on the ground. He nodded to the officers on foot and the two not occupied with Nadin went to the potion maker and checked her vitals.

"She's alive," said Adren. The lord waited for the officers to confirm, then nodded and sheathed his sword.

"I'm not here for you," he said.

"It doesn't matter. You can't have what you're after."

The lord chuckled. "I'm not after your unicorn, either."

"I know."

"Then why are you prepared to fight?"

The potion maker woke, saw the officers, and tried to make

a run for it. They grabbed her before she could get to her feet and held her fast.

"Why have you surrounded me?" asked Adren.

"A precaution. You are free to go." The lord waved a hand and the riders parted at the end of the circle opposite to him. Adren tried to discern what he was thinking, but his face remained impassive. Her mind raced to come up with something that would help in this situation that felt all too much like a trap. Lord Watorej had to know, if not from Nadin's yells, then from the lady's thanks, that Adren had been complicit in this.

"I'm not leaving without the unicorn."

"So tell it to follow."

Adren raised an eyebrow. "Sure. I'll just command it. That'll go over well."

The lord frowned and pressed his lips together. "So be it." He nodded at the riders and they headed out, the officers on foot following with their captives. The lord stayed, though, and waded into the inlet until the water was up to his shins. Adren relaxed her stance, but kept her knife out.

All he did was stand, feet shoulder-width apart, hands clasped behind his back. A soldier's pose, its formality softened by how he furrowed his brows and bit his lip as he stared across the water. Adren followed his gaze, but found nothing exceptional. Neither did he, it seemed, for he turned, pain etched into his face. Eyes red, he pushed back through the water, his shoes crunching on the gravel as he went to his horse. With a creak of the saddle and the swish of fabric across leather, he mounted the horse, but didn't immediately ride off. He paused, took a deep and deliberate breath, and then set out to the town.

Adren watched until long after he disappeared among the trees and listened until long after the hoofbeats died away before she put her knife away to search for the potion maker's object. Even if she didn't know how to use it, she would rather try than wait. If only she'd thought to see what it was before she threw it away! The forest floor, thick with moss as it was, provided few places to hide. The occasional smattering of ferns could give cover, and these Adren checked thoroughly. The holes, too, in and between decaying wood, could have become the resting place of the ill-fated throw. These were harder to search, requiring the displacement of dirt and rotten wood. Some, especially in the case of animal burrows, were simply too deep and narrow for Adren to search, or too fresh for her to risk sticking an arm in without being able to see what lay inside.

Lord Watorej had Nadin. The fact that he had the potion maker posed no problem to Adren and, in fact, would solve the issue of the possible threat against the unicorn, but the fact that he had Nadin was a different matter. Much as Adren wanted to leave once the unicorn had woken, much as she *could* leave, she knew she would regret it. As human as he was, Adren couldn't deny that he had still helped her, the unicorn, and the lady all he could. However small the magic part of him was, it existed, and he should not be punished for doing what was right.

Or should he? The tale he'd told about his mother had cut Adren to the core, and it might even be true, with what scant evidence Adren had. And yet, his own actions didn't line up. He said he'd worked hard to help his mother, and yet he had helped Adren with theft, leading into what could all too easily be seen as kidnapping Lord Watorej's wife, and the injury of the lord's horses. Add into that the potential that Nadin had, in fact, been stupid enough to be seen by the lord and his officers while using the magic he tried to hide, and the picture painted in Adren's mind held enough contradictions to be suspect. The woman who had called him at his house may have been his mother, and may even have been sick, but his story could have been hyperbole only. And, if he had lied about something like that, then Adren would know he couldn't be trusted any longer.

This is what Adren got for accepting his help. Trouble. Perhaps more than it was worth.

She pulled back a layer of bark, holding a fern to the side only to find another empty hollow.

Suppose Nadin had been honest, suppose he helped her out of a sense of duty and suppose his moral outrage over the lady's condition hadn't been faked. Suppose that he was really good enough to sacrifice his job for another's freedom. What would Lord Watorej do to him?

But there was another puzzle. Five years ago, the lord had trapped the lady to become his unwilling bride. Five years ago, his heart opened into a hole of unquenchable greed. Five years ago, he had broken his bargain with a shrewd and powerful potion maker who knew the value of magic, and who he now held, with Nadin, in his custody.

Perhaps the better question was not what Lord Watorej might do to Nadin, but what the potion maker might do to Nadin as she sought revenge against the lord. Or what she might do once she found out about Nadin's magic. He had been right to hide it. Whatever had really happened five years ago between Lord Watorej and the potion maker, Adren didn't doubt that the former's change in personality had everything to do with the latter's anger. How the potency of that anger might manifest around—or, saints forbid through—Nadin was something Adren didn't want to imagine.

There was nothing for it; she would have to go to his house and test him, see if he had told the truth about his mother. If so, then, for Nadin's sake, Adren would see what the unicorn could do. Nadin had tried everything he could buy, but no one could buy a unicorn. Not like this. The healing would only be an attempt, as Adren wasn't sure of the extent of the unicorn's abilities, especially with its madness. It could heal broken bones, knife wounds, and minor illnesses, that much Adren knew from experience, but even healthy unicorns had limits to their ability. If only the potion maker had really had a cure! Still, there was no use hoping for something that wouldn't happen. She could make do with what she had.

Adren paused, hand partway down a burrow, to stare into the masked face of a raccoon. It drew back, hair raised. She also drew back to resume the search... elsewhere.

Light. That was what she needed. The raccoon had been sleeping and she must have woken it. A rude shock that, and no wonder it had come up to investigate. But if she had some way to light up these burrows, checking them would be both easier and safer, for all parties.

Her magic hummed beneath her skin. It had yet to infiltrate every corner of her, but it had begun to nestle in, at which points it gave off nervous energy, a growing desire to be used. To think that Nadin had this flowing through him all the time! Adren had no idea how he dealt with it. He'd been born with it, fair enough, but it must drive him crazy at least some of the time. Perhaps, in time, she would become used to the feel of it in her bones. Or perhaps using it made its presence more bearable.

This was why she needed to find the object. Not only might she be able to wake the unicorn, but she would also be able to get a feel for controlled magic, which she could then replicate. A baby may have legs, but it still took time to learn how to walk.

By the time the sun started to dip below the horizon, Adren had still not found the object. She sat next to the unicorn, arms wrapped around her knees. Index finger out, she let a tiny bit of magic outside of it and tried to make light. All it did was give off a faint perfume. The rest rushed within her, strained against her control, and it took almost all she had to keep only that smallest thread dancing against her skin. Where had this magic come from? The dark part in her mind, yes, but had that part always been there? Had she been born with it, or had it been when—?

No. Adren stopped the release of magic and shut her eyes. Not those thoughts. Not that time.

The unicorn stirred beside her and she opened her eyes to see that the sky had darkened considerably. She stood and placed a gentle hand on the unicorn's shoulder. Its eyes were still closed, but she felt its weight shift as its hind leg lowered. A shiver passed through its body and, before that passed, it lifted its head and its eyelids parted. Through the connection, it was as if ripples had passed over water and the unicorn's emotions shone clear again. They spiked into panic, but calmed as Adren rubbed the unicorn's neck. Confusion reigned, but not fear. Adren continued to stroke its neck and smiled.

"Thou hast victory over thy dreams," she whispered before she hugged it and let all the tension drain out of her. Part of her had doubted the potion maker's claim that the unicorn would wake at sundown, was sure that only magic would wake it. The unicorn flinched as she brushed against the still-tender lines on its flank. She drew away. "Now, dear one, I have need of thee and thy magic." She beckoned and started towards the town, filling herself with as much expectancy and excitement as she could muster. The unicorn hesitated but, after some coaxing, it came up beside her and didn't try to depart.

Chapter Nine

The sky had grown dark by the time they entered the town, Adren keeping a hand on the unicorn's flank so she could hold it invisible. The streets were empty for all intents and purposes, but Adren kept an eye and an ear out for disturbances while she walked as if she didn't have an elk-sized unicorn following right next to her. She took her time and stopped often to renew the invisibility, or to redirect the unicorn when it got sidetracked or spooked at something blown in a gust of wind. After all, they had the whole night. It didn't matter that the unicorn was fascinated by the street lamps and their halos of buzzing insects, and would try to spear the largest bugs on its horn. Adren hadn't brought the unicorn into a town or city for a long time, she realized. It likely remembered little about them. So much the better.

When they arrived at Nadin's house, all the doors were locked and closed, even the entrance to the barn. Adren put an ear to it, but all was silent within. Who would lock an empty building? She shook her head. Humans really did operate outside the realm of logic. The barn didn't even have stalls in it.

"If I ever grow to understand humans," she said to the unicorn, "please, put me out of my misery." Then she turned her attention to the lock. It was unusual, of complicated make. The locks on the door to the house were the same, and none of the windows presented any option quieter than breaking them. Of course, these happened to be not only well above floor level, but also too small for anything other than a cat to fit through. One thing she could say for Nadin was he knew how to keep away unwanted visitors. She knocked on the front door. Nothing.

Adren had expected security. She hadn't expected that no one would come to the door. If Nadin's mother really were as sick as he'd said, wouldn't there be someone to watch her?

Well, that was the front. Time to check the back. Adren turned to leave, but the unicorn didn't follow. Instead, it stuck its horn into the lock and wiggled it a bit. Then it pulled back and stepped away, stretching its nose towards the door.

"That's not how a lock works." But the unicorn stamped its foot and refused to come with her. Sighing, Adren went back to the lock and pulled at it. It opened without difficulty. Mouth agape, Adren stared at the unicorn. It responded by arching its neck and feeling smug, the sentiment radiating shamelessly through their connection. She wished it could tell her where it had learned how to do that. And how it had learned that, considering the difficulties she had teaching it.

They entered the barn, Adren closing the door behind them with as little noise as possible. She put a hand on the unicorn's nose and made herself feel content, hoping it would understand that she wanted it to stay in the barn. Houses were built only with humans in mind, and Adren wanted to make sure the unicorn would be able to follow her before she had to lead it. That, and if Nadin's mother weren't as sick as he'd said, then she and the unicorn would be able to leave at once. The unicorn lay down in the middle of the barn and stared up at Adren, head tilted. She almost giggled at it, but controlled herself.

She put her ear to the inner door to the house and counted slowly to ten, alert to the sound of movement. Hearing none, she opened the door and walked inside.

The curtains on the barn windows let in so much light from the street lamps that they could be removed and make little difference. This light, although hampered by the inner door, spread into the house and allowed Adren to make her way to the stairs without tripping over anything. Good locks, but threadbare curtains. Adren didn't know what to make of that.

The staircase was dark, though, and ghoulish with shadows. Adren pretended that each step was really a goblin or demon in disguise and that she had to let her weight down gradually so the creature would not know someone stepped on it. Otherwise, it would scream and give her away. She couldn't remember where she had gotten this from, but the memory felt old and very familiar. There had been a pair of blue eyes and a high, clear laugh that sounded every time she fumbled on the steps. There was no face, though. There were never any faces.

Adren let the memory vanish from her mind. She climbed the last few stairs and left behind the moment of pretending. It was much better to deal with what she could experience through her senses rather than the conjurations of her mind.

Now, which room had Nadin gone to when he had answered his mother's call? The first, most likely. Adren slipped the door open to peek inside. A large bed stood against the far wall and on the bed lay a woman nearing middle age. The light from her window illuminated her face, lines etched by pain standing out in sharp contrast due to the angle of the shadows. She moaned and, as she turned over onto her side, Adren noted a sheen of sweat on her forehead and the greyness of her skin. Unless this was some kind of elaborate deception, Nadin had told the truth of the physical nature of his mother's illness. But Adren did not think it a deception. As Nadin's mother turned over again in her bed, it seemed to Adren that she could see another woman, pale with sickness and on the verge of death, and she could feel her heart breaking for that woman. She shook her head and the memory evaporated, but the emotion remained.

Leaving the door ajar, Adren returned to the unicorn. She beckoned to it and it followed, squeezing through the doorway as it entered the house. When she went up the stairs, it stopped at the bottom and sniffed at them, disapproval clear as it turned an ear to the staircase. Adren gestured at it to come, and it climbed with delicate steps. It felt foolish and seemed keen to make sure Adren knew it, but she didn't stop or turn back.

Once they had arrived at the second floor, she led it into the room. It stared at Nadin's mother for a long moment, emotions in turmoil. Then it went up to her and placed its horn on her forehead. Nadin's mother turned, frowning. The unicorn kept its horn in place. It stayed like that, tail swishing. Nadin's mother muttered and sat up, startling the unicorn, who stepped back into the wall and tossed its head. The woman's wild eyes opened, her focus at once on Adren and the unicorn.

"Demons!" she cried, her voice shrill. "You spawn of the occult come to kill me! Get out! You two may have my health but you cannot take my life. Get *out!*" She flung herself against the back wall, clinging to her own head and weeping. "No, no, no… they can't have come here; they can't have found me. I was too careful. I've always been too careful." Then she shuddered and her voice became harsh. "But they found me already. How else am I sick? *Get out!* Twins are always a sign, but he wasn't careful, not like I was. None of them were careful, but I am alive."

Something about those words bypassed Adren's mind and stuck in her body, caused her heart to pound. It had to be because this was the first time she'd ever been in the same room as an insane human. Had to be. Saints, she hadn't been prepared for this. She'd had no idea it would be this bad. The unicorn's fear crept through the connection with icy hands, and the chill of it echoed within Adren. Shaking her head to rid herself of the feeling, Adren put an arm around the unicorn's neck and pulled it from the room. Nadin's mother continued ranting, muffled by her own hands and then the door, as a stinging pain started in the middle of Adren's forehead. She led the unicorn down to the stairs and out through the barn, then closed the lock and made sure it had fastened before they left.

No wonder Nadin had hated seeing the lady mistreated.

Sweet saints, it was as if someone had swiped a sword across Adren's forehead and taken off the skin. She touched the place, but it had no effect on the pain. Bah. It would go away before long. She ignored it and focused instead on keeping the unicorn invisible as they made their way back to the forest.

The unicorn halted at a crossroad, so abruptly that Adren almost lost contact with it. It stood, every muscle taut, staring down the street that went back roughly in the direction of the potion maker's shop. The unicorn's terror vibrated at the back of her mind, more intense even than what it had felt just before the spell had begun to take hold. Adren scanned the street, but couldn't see what had caused this.

"There is nothing," she said, gentle in tone and feeling. "Nothing to frighten thee." But the unicorn began to shake, its emotions unaffected by hers for the first time in years. It made a low moaning sound she had not thought it capable of making, and then an echo of feeling ran through it. As it grew, Adren recognized it as a reliving of the potion maker's spell. Oh, no. This must have been where it happened. She had taken so long to convince it to stop coming after her, she should have had some idea of where it had been when it stopped. And to be trapped by the potion maker so soon after… how the unicorn had come through the town and how the potion maker trapped it without causing a commotion, Adren didn't know, but it didn't matter. Right now, it needed her.

The unicorn's shaking continued as the echo of paralysis crept up and through it. Making sure the streets were empty, Adren let go of the invisibility and hugged the unicorn's neck.

"She is gone, and powerless. Thou canst not be caught by her again. I promise thee." She let the memory of the spell wash over herself as well, became a mirror to the unicorn. Its remembered experience fell into the same rhythm and potency as hers and it was as if they were both the same creature in that moment. The ghost of the spell moved to subdue everything in its path until it arrived, in Adren's mind, at the dark place. She let herself experience again how the spell had cracked the barrier. This caught the unicorn's attention. Its memory paused as it listened to her experience. The crack slivered itself open again, the magic flowed through it to overwhelm the spell with its power.

This caused the unicorn's shaking to become more violent as it tried to assert its memory over hers, tried to make her feel what it had felt, but Adren held fast. The magic within her helped, heightening her reliving of its release and its victory until the unicorn let its memory of the spell wash away with hers, leaving only calm behind. Its muscles relaxed and it bent to nudge her with its nose, grateful. Adren gave its neck a tiny squeeze.

Through all this, the stinging in Adren's forehead hadn't stopped. If anything, it had grown worse. Now her whole head throbbed with it, making it difficult to think. She kneaded her forehead in an effort to encourage it to go away.

They only made it a block before she had to halt and try to deal with... whatever was happening. There was no injury, and the unicorn's horn did nothing, and yet the pain remained.

Adren was about to let the unicorn become visible again and let her chest relax when five people came down the street, voices slurred and gaits unsteady. One of them, a skinny man who seemed the leader, saw Adren and pointed at her, laughing.

"Can't hold your drink, can you?" He then proceeded to trip over his own feet.

Adren put her hand to her side and walked again, her steps quick. She had waited too long to renew the invisibility, and now the tightness in her chest made it hard to breathe. Her magic only made this more acute; it pounded in her ears now, screamed at her to use it.

The skinny man regained his footing and followed after her. Adren walked faster, but he kept up and leaned in towards her, grinning as his friends yelled at him incoherently.

"You come with me, and I'll show you how it's done." His breath stank of alcohol. Without looking at him, Adren raised a hand and wiggled her middle fingers. If she spoke, she might lose her hold on both the invisibility and the magic. All she had to do was get past them without causing an incident. She could do that. The unicorn did a nervous dance beside her and she had to sway to keep in contact with it. The man spat at her, missing her hand by a hair's breadth and hitting her shoulder instead.

"That was rude," he growled. Then he reached out to grab Adren with unsteady arms. She couldn't move fast enough and he pulled her towards him, breaking her contact with the unicorn. His eyes widened when it appeared and his friends became dead silent. Adren wrenched herself free, her chest aching. Please let them be drunk enough to laugh it off. Or something similarly harmless.

"The hell is that?" yelled one of his friends.

"I think we're drunk," said the man, looking more stunned than anything else. "It's not real." If she just walked away...

"You said that this morning, too, when we were sober. I think it *is* real." Gods. And, as she realized the implications of 'this morning': in hell.

"Wait," said the man as he grabbed Adren's arm. "We need to figure out if it's real." He tried to push her out of the way, but she freed herself and stepped back towards the unicorn. Her forehead burned. It interfered with her ability to think, but not so much that she didn't understand what was happening. They had seen the unicorn earlier that day. They had seen it, right when the potion maker had captured it, and they had done nothing to help. The magic within her pulsed in sync with her forehead and though it nearly caused her to lose her balance every time it strengthened, she welcomed it. She almost fell back against the unicorn, staying upright out of sheer will. For its sake, she had to stay in control of herself. The skinny man lunged at her when she could do nothing to block him and punched her in the stomach. Adren doubled over, more to stop the magic than the pain, though his blow had been solid. Her whole self was nearly infiltrated by this power. It had only a few corners left to fill.

The skinny man's friends had caught up to them by this point and stood behind him, an audience. They cheered when he punched Adren, yelling encouragement at him.

The unicorn shied away from the skinny man and stood in place, stamping at the ground. Adren wanted it to do something, but it was too scared and she knew it. Likely it couldn't understand what it felt from her, which only made it worse.

She tried to direct her emotions and, by extension, the unicorn, but she couldn't. Focus too much on that, and the magic made its move. Suppress the magic and watch her self-control slip. She didn't know how long she could keep this balancing act up.

"You know, I think you're right," the skinny man said to his friends as he approached the unicorn. He tripped on an uneven patch on the road and pitched forward onto the unicorn. His hands flailed until they found something to hold onto: the unicorn's still-healing flesh. Both the unicorn and Adren screamed as his hands dug into the wounds. The unicorn took off at once, leaving the man to fall on his face. But Adren could not run. The last place had been settled. The magic had finished its work in her and nothing could suppress its roar to be released.

Now, with her horned companion gone, Adren didn't care anymore what happened to these drunks who had watched the unicorn in pain and done nothing. Or rather, she did care. She cared quite a bit.

It didn't take much to let her magic explode.

Chapter Ten

When Adren came to, she found herself lying on a bed in a bedroom that would not look out of place in Lord Watorej's mansion. Unless there was someone else who would put two vanity tables in the same room.

Gods in hell.

The magic inside her had melted into a gentle background presence. As much as she didn't regret letting it loose, Adren hoped in the name of every saint that it would stay this subdued for the rest of her life. It did bother her, though, that she couldn't seem to remember what the aftermath of her magic had been.

She got out of bed and went to the window. It was both locked and barred, although that didn't keep it from letting in morning light. Aside from that, she was on the third floor of the mansion and there was nothing visible that she'd be able to use to climb down. Next to try was the door, which was also locked. Beneath it, she could see the shoes of whoever had been set to guard her. She sat back on the bed and searched the room for something she could use as a weapon. The furniture consisted of two vanities, an empty bookshelf, various paintings, one large wardrobe and one smaller one, and the bed. Upon opening what could be opened, Adren discovered that all the contents of the drawers had been removed, and the large wardrobe contained only a used handkerchief. Wrinkling her nose at it, she closed the wardrobe before returning to the bed.

The question at this moment was less how she would escape and more where Nadin was and how she would get the both of them out of there. She could throw the handkerchief under the door and scare the guard away with uncleanliness. Yes. That would definitely work. No doubt about it.

The door opened and Lord Watorej entered. Adren stood.

"How are you?" he asked. His concern appeared genuine.

"Locked up."

"I didn't want you to run away. I need your help."

"With what?" She watched without moving as he sat down on the bed and gestured for her to do the same.

"It's something of a long story."

"I can stand. You can make it short."

He sighed and stared at his hands. For a moment, he was silent, and Adren could tell from the way he would move his lips every once in a while only to grimace that he was trying to figure out how he was going to explain himself.

"I'm cursed. My wife—she didn't do it—but..." His hands balled into fists. Then he took a deep breath and tried again. "A little over five years ago, I fell in love with a selkie woman, but she didn't want me like I wanted her. So, I made a bargain with the potion maker. Once I had the selkie, though, I didn't fulfill my end of the bargain, and so she and I were cursed. She started to forget who she was, and I became controlled by my possessions. You freed her, which I could not do because of my curse, but now I am left behind. So, when I discovered you had magic, I had you brought here. Will you free me from this?"

A curse? That explained a lot.

Adren took a moment to process his story. So, he hadn't been responsible for the lady's forgetting. Well, not like she'd thought. And he'd kidnapped the lady, although that had been clear from what she'd said. Although, as he said, she was free now. Adren could escape with Nadin without having to ever touch this curse Lord Watorej had clearly brought upon himself.

Except for the fact that Nadin had made it clear he didn't want to leave town. His mother wouldn't be able to travel, after all. He would only be imprisoned again.

This was nonsense. Even if Adren wanted to, she couldn't break the curse. She couldn't even make light! And Nadin had magic, too, under much better control than hers. Oh gods, and Lord Watorej would have talked to him about this when she'd been left with the unicorn, which meant Nadin had already refused for who knew what reason. Fine. She'd escape and go get him. He needed someone to talk sense into him.

"No."

The lord's face fell, but only for an instant before fury bloomed, as if something other than himself had taken his features and twisted them into what it wanted him to feel.

"Then I will let neither you nor Nadin leave this mansion for as long as I have breath. You have taken what is mine and so I have taken you."

At this, Adren had to laugh. "Yours? You think that she and her sealskin were yours? Must you be so saintsall stupid?"

Lord Watorej started at the swearing. "Do you know who I am?" he asked quietly.

"Of course. You're the idiot who kidnapped a selkie and forced her to marry him, broke his agreement with his accomplice and got cursed by her, and now thinks I'll help to break that curse. And if you think you can keep me caged here, that only proves how little you know me."

"I know you stole a substantial amount of money from my vault with the help of magic. The particularly antagonized owner of a dye shop was only too happy to inform my officers of the pale young woman who came in, threatened her, and left with black and brown dye. And, with that rather spectacular display last night, I knew who you were. The cash in your coat pocket only confirmed it. Am I still stupid?"

Adren didn't move. She wouldn't give him the satisfaction of checking her pockets.

"Granted, if you still refuse," the lord continued, "I might

110

find that unicorn of yours and see what I can make it do. A potion maker of our mutual acquaintance informs me it would be simple." While the connections he'd made about her identity as the thief hadn't impressed her much—she *had* had the money in her pocket, after all—the fact that the potion maker had begun to make good on her promise made Adren's muscles clench.

"If you or anyone in your service comes anywhere near the unicorn, you'd better pray that the gods don't take too much of an interest in you. The saints won't be letting you into heaven when I kill you." If he or his servants had taken the money, they had almost certainly also taken her knife, so she didn't reach to her hip, but she didn't need to. Her words were blade enough.

"I see. You need time." Lord Watorej walked to the door. "While you decide, know this: Nadin has worked for me for a few years now and, from all I've heard of his supervisors and the other mechanics, his character is impeccable. I've heard rumours that you have some sort of hold over him, which may explain your alliance, but I have chosen not to believe them. For now. And, since it seems you do care about more than just yourself, I feel the need to inform you that, if those rumours are true, you are playing with both the reputation and future of a very good man. You should consider that."

"You should consider the possibility *he* did nothing wrong."

"Neither did I." He knocked on the door and the servant guarding it—the footman, of all people—let him out. The two of them spoke a moment before he left, their voices too quiet for Adren to make out the words.

Nadin was in the mansion, was he? That was… convenient.

There was also the matter of the footman. Lord Watorej had officers, and probably also a private prison. Why lock them up in the mansion with servants as guards? He couldn't be that idiotic, although it could be the curse. Adren wasn't sure, but she wasn't about to sit around trying to figure it out. She had a mansion to escape from and a Nadin to rescue. Not necessarily in that order.

So, she began her work. The windows may have been locked up tight, but that didn't mean they couldn't be useful. When

Adren checked the drawers on the vanity tables again, she found that she could remove them. This she did with care, lest she disturb the footman too soon. Then she tied together bedsheets and anchored one end to the bed. There weren't enough to get her to the ground, but her guard didn't need to know that. She brought them to the window and set them in easy reach as she hefted a drawer. If she hit the lock just so...

She missed the lock, but she hit the window and it cracked. Close enough. With a solid crash against the glass, it shattered.

Outside the door, keys jangled and the footman muttered to himself. Quick, quick.

Adren threw the bedsheet rope through the hole in the window and turned herself invisible. The footman entered the room, did a double take, and gaped.

"That's not possible!"

As he approached the window, Adren came up behind him and made her move. One arm went around the neck, hand grasping above the opposite elbow. The other hand pressed his head down as she squeezed. By the end of a nine-count, he went limp. Adren grabbed his keys and locked the door behind her.

Before she could relax, however, there was a shout from the other end of the hallway. Another footman stood by a door, face white. She let herself become visible and made a face at him. He paused, then ran at her. She waited, waited, waited, for just the right moment—then stepped out of the way. And kicked him, for good measure. He fell flat on his face. When he tried to get up, his nose all bloody, Adren punched him and he went down again. His pockets contained several keys, which she took to the door he'd been guarding to try them on its lock.

The footman in her room should have woken by now and started banging on the door or shouting, or both. Someone from nearby should have heard the other footman's shout and come to his aid. There should have been another guard or two on each of the doors, all now trying to stop her. And yet, the hall remained silent. Adren was having an inkling.

But, first, the lock.

"It's the brass one," Nadin said through the door after she'd tried and failed with four keys. Adren opened her mouth to make a sarcastic retort, but he spoke before she could: "Sorry, I didn't realize it was you right away." She satisfied herself with rolling her eyes and unlocking the door. Nadin more or less ran out of the room, then stopped halfway down the hallway and turned around with a puzzled look.

"Lord Watorej has set a trap," she informed him.

"Hell." The corners of Nadin's mouth drooped. "Do you know what it is?"

"Certainly. I can read his mind." Adren raised an eyebrow. Nadin raised his hands.

"I was just asking. If you could tell he has a trap, who knows what else you'd figured out? What do we do?"

"Escape. The easy way or the hard way."

"What's the hard way?" he asked, cringing. Odd. Hadn't Lord Watorej spoken to him about the curse? No, Nadin must share her desire to deal with the worst side before the best. Oh, sweet saints, had she just likened that boy to herself? Ugh. Never again. It felt too uncomfortable.

"Resist your lord at every step."

"Isn't that generally how escapes work?"

"Or you could break the curse that's on him."

Nadin's eyes grew round. "The what?"

Saints. Nadin had managed to keep his magic secret after all.

"The potion maker put a curse on him because she had helped him get the lady and he didn't honour his side of their agreement. He asked me to break it, and I refused. We can leave easily if it's broken. You might have to move to a different town if it isn't." There. Simple. Straightforward. Adren had no idea how the lord had taken any longer to explain it himself.

"Why did he ask you? You don't have that kind of magic. Do you?" Adren wondered whether she should tell him about the change in her. No, he didn't need to know. They wouldn't see each other again after this.

"What you really should be asking is why he didn't ask you.

113

I didn't tell him you could do it, seeing as you seem to be trying to keep your magic secret."

"And you're not?"

"Not actively. Will you do it?"

Nadin bit his lower lip. The footman on the ground stirred and they both froze, but he soon grew still again.

"Yes. I'll do it."

With some effort, they woke the footman and asked him to bring them to Lord Watorej. He was a little fuzzy when he came to, but that wore off before too long and he was able to take them straight to the lord. He and five security officers waited for them in the main entrance to the mansion. Why he expected them to attempt escape through the front entrance, Adren didn't know. But he'd said he wasn't stupid, so...

"Why are you *both* here?" asked Lord Watorej with a frown.

"My lord, I can break your curse," Nadin blurted out as his tongue almost tripped over itself in his rush to say the words.

Elegant.

"But you're a mechanic." The lord crossed his arms. Adren held her tongue.

"I can still do magic. I'm the one who got the sealskin out of the clock in the library, not her. I can break the curse." Nadin's voice trembled and Adren could see that his hands shook. She hoped that what he was afraid of was only in his mind.

"If you can, then by all means..." Eyebrow raised, Lord Watorej spread his hands.

Nadin nodded, swallowed, and took a deep breath. After almost too long a pause, he spoke, his hands shaking even more.

"I can't see it."

Oh, no. That was a mistake, trying to see a curse. Spells could be seen by those with Nadin's ability but curses, their opposite, could not. Adren was baffled as to how Nadin didn't know something this basic.

"You can't see what?" the lord growled. Nadin bit his lip.

"I can't see the magic that made the curse. I... usually can see magic... I can't right now. It's not because I'm distracted or too focused"—he directed that comment at Adren—"but it's like there's nothing for me to see."

"Are you telling me you can't do this?"

"No, he's not," Adren cut in before Nadin could make the situation worse. Her words were for him, but she spoke to the lord and hoped he would understand. "He's only confirmed that it really is a curse. If it had been a spell, he would see the added magic, but curses take away." Nadin frowned, then raised his eyebrows in surprise... which turned into fear. He shook his head, which earned a glare from her. If he could open the clock, he could deal with a curse. There really was no question about it.

"My lord, I need to speak with Adren in private."

"You may not." Lord Watorej crossed his arms. Adren considered the possibility of her and Nadin running right then, but a quick glance behind showed that eight more officers had come around back. She might be able to escape, but Nadin wouldn't. The lord addressed Adren. "Stop wasting my time with this nonsense. It's clear that Nadin only says this because you've pressured him. Now, either you remove my curse or you will suffer the consequences of stealing from nobility. I don't understand why you refuse to do what will gain your freedom."

"Because she can't! I'm the one with the magic, not her." At Nadin's outcry, Lord Watorej nodded to his officers, two of which grabbed Nadin and covered his mouth as they pulled him back. When he calmed, they took their hands from his mouth, but they didn't let him go. Knowing Nadin, if Adren had been the one to grab him, she would have kept him gagged, but she decided not to enlighten the officers.

"Your hold over him will not help here," said the lord.

"If you needed my help so badly, why didn't you ask when you first met me?"

"You had a knife out and were accompanied by a unicorn. It seemed you would be disinclined to help. And I needed proof that you could do magic. Last night provided that proof."

"Proof of the wrong thing. I may have magic, but it's the wrong kind for curse-breaking." Well, in her hands, it was.

"You burned three people and blinded two others."

"You *what?*"

That, apparently.

"Why didn't you keep your end of your bargain with the potion maker?" Adren said, ignoring Nadin's outburst.

Lord Watorej grimaced. "She wanted me to let her control the selkie one day a week for as many weeks as she needed. I couldn't let her."

"Because you wanted to control the selkie yourself."

"I loved her! She was mine!" He couldn't seem to keep his hands still.

"Oh, sure you did. Forcing someone to marry you is the very definition of love."

Lord Watorej paled. Nearly all his officers shifted position, giving him an uncertain look.

"I didn't sleep with her!" the lord yelled. Adren raised an eyebrow. First of all, she didn't believe that he'd done nothing with his wife in five years of marriage and, second, neither would his officers. Not if they had any intelligence. Lady Watorej had been right when she wondered who among the humans would accept their union. According to some, the saints put a stop to the intermixing of humans and magical creatures when they defeated the gods and, included within their group, were those who believed that the children of such unions were, if not outright demonic, then deformed in spirit. Not that demons existed, but that was something for magicians to argue over. Plenty of humans believed in them, Nadin's mother being one of them, considering her ranting. Did she know about Nadin's abilities? Adren hadn't considered that. But enough.

"Never mind what you didn't do with your wife. You—"

"Stop. Stop with all this second-guessing and this stalling. I don't know why I'm going along with your games when I am the one with the power here. Break the curse. Now. You're the only one here who can do it and I will wait no longer. I may not deserve it in your eyes, but I will have it." His voice grew fierce and he stepped towards Adren, his body erect and chin raised.

"I can't." A chill entered the tips of her fingers.

"You mean you won't."

"No, you idiot. I can't. I can't break your curse." The officers shrank back from Lord Watorej at her insult, but he didn't say anything. His gaze seemed to turn inwards, and he became still. In the stillness, Adren noticed that her chest felt tight, like it did when she held her invisibility in place.

"Adren," Nadin said, "what about the...?" He mouthed the word 'unicorn' before the officers could suppress him. Unfortunately, the lord saw and heard everything.

"Perhaps I should follow the potion maker's advice. She said the unicorn and you had some sort of connection, that it would come if you called. Or were hurt." He tapped his chin.

The tightness in Adren's chest had grown, and cold had spread up her arms, as if her veins had begun to freeze. Nadin shouldn't have said that. Shouldn't have endangered the unicorn. Shouldn't have been stupid. If that's what it had been.

She was finding it hard to breathe.

Lord Watorej would go after the unicorn now, for certain. He would hunt it, he would hurt it. He might even make another bargain with the potion maker. She would put the spell on it, and Adren would feel everything. This had to be stopped.

As the ice travelled to her shoulders and down her body, it occurred to Adren that something might be happening to her. Perhaps a spell. No, because then her magic would fight it. So something else. The mansion's lamps, probably. They were so bright. Everything was so bright. And the space so cramped— had the ceiling lowered? The walls come nearer?

The lord was frowning at her. How long had it been since he spoke? She should say something. But her chest hurt so much. Her heart had so little room left, it had to beat faster to make up for it. Breathe, Adren, breathe. It didn't help. No matter how much she needed it to help, it didn't.

"Adren?"

Shut up, Nadin.

Adren's forehead tingled, stabbed. Her veins had frozen

completely. Despite the fact that she'd shut her eyes and covered her ears, everything was getting worse. Fast. And she couldn't hide it from the unicorn. The unicorn! No, no, no, it couldn't feel what she was feeling. It would come after her. It would come here, right in the midst of Lord Watorej's power. Nadin just had to have to mentioned it.

Get a hold of yourself, Adren. But she couldn't get a hold of herself. She felt control slipping from her, just as her emotions flew through the connection and the unicorn started to run. And, with every throb of her heart and her forehead, the dark place in her mind throbbed, too. It rattled in place, just another of too many things moving at once, more than she had hands to stop them. The only thing that could be moving that wasn't was her magic, but that only made it worse. What if it were causing everything and no matter what she did, no matter how hard she tried, she would never be able to stop this?

The unicorn.

The unicorn was coming.

She couldn't stop it, and she needed to.

Adren opened her eyes. Everything was still too bright, and she may not be able to stop the unicorn, but she thought she could get it where it might have an advantage, so she squinted.

"You want the unicorn?" she said to Lord Watorej. "Get me to the forest. Now."

Chapter Eleven

They went in a motorized cart, in part for speed and in part because Adren couldn't manage to walk. Nadin sat on one side of her, and an officer sat on the other. She directed Lord Watorej by pointing, although she had closed her eyes again so that she didn't have to hate every single bump on the road. Whatever was happening to her body calmed a bit, giving her hope, only for everything to start again as they reached the edge of the town. This time it was worse and she was certain that, if she couldn't get herself under control, she might stop being able to breathe.

"Adren." Nadin. "Adren, can you walk?"

No.

She didn't even want to walk. She wanted to curl up somewhere, somewhere quiet and dark. Maybe she wouldn't die if she could do that.

Except she couldn't do that, she remembered. They were still in town, the unicorn wasn't safe yet, and there wasn't much time. If only there weren't so many images and sounds and sensations floating up from and falling back into the dark place in her mind. They made it hard to think.

Nadin ended up carrying her—she wasn't sure how that was sorted out, but it helped to feel his arms supporting her. It kept her inside her body and the panic out.

"You're heavier than I thought you were," he said, but quietly. Probably so the others wouldn't be able to hear.

"H-have to be," she managed to get out. "I had to beat up a lot of people here."

"Yeah, and two of them were me." Adren didn't need to see him to know he was grinning. It was all through his voice. She wanted to laugh. "Did you really burn three people? And blind two?" He sounded worried.

"The reports... of my abilities... are greatly exaggerated." Which was true, in a way.

"Oh."

"Why are you... really helping me?" she asked, to keep him talking as much as to know the answer. It didn't work all that well. Nadin paused for a long time. But then he spoke.

"I'm not very good at helping people, but when I saw you and the unicorn, I thought maybe..." His voice cracked. "I thought maybe I could finally make a difference."

Honeysuckle sweetness spread over Adren's tongue, warming it a little, and her chest didn't feel quite so tight.

"Keep talking," she said.

He told her about his childhood, before his mother was sick and when the livery barn was still up and running. Their neighbours complained about the smell of the manure, so they made an agreement with the farmers south of town, and sometimes Nadin would help bring it down. His favourite part of the trip, right up there with the fresh milk, was seeing the machines some of the wealthier farmers used in their work. When his mother got too sick to work, he tried to keep the business going, but didn't have the head for it. Or the maturity. He wasn't sure what had caused them, but after one too many bad decisions, he was forced to close the barn and sell what he had left. Thankfully, his fascination with farming equipment had given him enough knowledge to gain his current position as a mechanic. It wasn't ideal, but it paid enough for him and his mother to live, and for him to treat her illness as best he could.

"No father?" Adren asked.

"No."

From the crack in the dark place came a memory of a man in black who knelt by the bedside of a woman, kissing her cheek as tears ran down his face. When it faded from Adren's conscious mind, the magic caught at it and it left traces. The kiss, his clothing, the tears. She wished she knew where they were from.

"I guess the reason I kept helping you," Nadin said, "was because you expect me to be able to do things. You don't let me sit around and feel sorry for myself when things aren't working, and you don't treat me like a failure. I wanted to say thank you for it earlier, but with everything happening, well, it was a little hard." He chuckled.

Adren's chest relaxed and her breath with it, enough that she thought she might not die just yet. Her body unclenched. Not completely, but enough.

"I can walk again," she said.

"Not yet," he said, his voice so quiet now that it was barely a murmur. "I overheard Lord Watorej say something yesterday on the way to the mansion."

"Make it quick. We've almost reached the unicorn."

"He and the potion maker were arguing about something. I couldn't hear everything because they were keeping it down and I was a bit ahead of them—I should have turned my head but I thought someone would notice and stop me—"

"Nadin. Quick. Rabbit-like."

"Lord Watorej said something like 'I let her go, but nothing changed' and 'of course she's what I want most' and then the potion maker said something about the unicorn and how she could help him get it. Do you think that has to do with the curse?"

A back door. Of course. Taking away with magic strains both the magic and its user, but if there's a backdoor, a way for things to return without more magic, then the taking isn't permanent. It made curses easier, and more gratifying if you designed the backdoor such that the curse itself prevented the afflicted from being able to use it. For the lady, it must have been getting her skin back, which would have meant not only remembering who she was, but also going against the lord's curse. The lord, being controlled by his possessions, as he said, would never give up the sealskin, especially if it meant giving up the thing he thought he wanted most: the lady. And the potion maker, wanting him to suffer, had told Lord Watorej that giving up what he wanted most would break the curse, and that the curse made that impossible. Given long enough, the lord would have had to bend to her demands in order to be free again.

But, if the lord didn't want the lady most of all things, then what *did* he really want?

Before she'd left, the lady had said to him: 'You are a child who thinks love means all must sacrifice at his altar.' After which he'd given her up, as he'd said. So it wasn't as impossible as he thought.

"Nadin."

"What?"

"I'm going to try something that might not work. If it doesn't, I'll still be able to leave, but won't be able to save you. Will you still help me?"

"Of course."

Sweetness on the tongue.

"Stop!" Lord Watorej called, his voice a spear through Adren's head. She went to put her hands on her ears again, but Nadin stopped her and put her down.

Wild confusion shot through from the unicorn. When Adren opened her eyes, she saw the lord, sword drawn, the officers around him with weapons out, and the unicorn before them, head lowered and horn ready. Adren's heart pounded. They would hurt it they would hurt it they would hurt it. She ran to the unicorn and, for some reason, the officers didn't stop her.

"You promised it would free me!" Lord Watorej cried, then started to call out an order.

"No, my lord." Nadin's voice was firm. "She needs to calm it. If you stop her, it'll attack, and that won't end well for any of us."

The unicorn raised its head as Adren came to it. She clung to its legs and slid to the ground. It didn't matter what Nadin said, the lord wanted the unicorn—no, he needed it—and he would take it. But it wouldn't do what he wanted, so he would kill it, use its horn for himself and sell the rest. That's what they all wanted. To hurt it. To murder it. To take a knife and stab it in its side right when it thought it was safe. Gain. That's all they cared about, these humans. And when they took the unicorn and had crushed all they could out of it, they would come for her. They would come for her and they would try to make her do what they wanted, so they would sell her. They would break her. They would give her to people who would touch her in ways no one had a right to touch her, all because she was "exotic." She remembered the ropes around her, the whisper in her ear as Pider told her exactly what all those ways were.

She remembered being jumped in the dark.

And the punch into more darkness.

She remembered how tightly she held onto the invisibility.

The pulse of battle.

Their connection as it fought.

And the knife.

Except, this time, it was a sword, and it wasn't just one man. Her hands shook as she clutched the unicorn, and she couldn't stop them. Her throat closed. This was it. No matter what she did now, it would all fall apart. There was nothing she could do to stop it. Nothing she could do to control it.

The unicorn's horn was cool on her cheek. Fear came through the connection, as did the heartbeat of violence, throb for throb with what Adren remembered only too well. Followed by the aftermath. And a calm, an assurance more silk than steel, of peace. A comforting touch. She found herself humming. It was a lullaby, but she couldn't seem to remember the words.

Terror. Away, away!

But only for a moment. The comfort was back. All was well.

No, all was not well. There was danger now, hiding in the shadows. Hiding in the light.

It is gone. All is well.

That's because you can't see it. I know, I know it's there.

All is well.

How?

Because I am with you.

The fog cleared from Adren's mind. Bit by bit, her heart slowed and she could breathe again. She could open her eyes and her ears without pain. She could stand. An echo of music threaded through her mind from the dark place, along with the image of a young girl who danced to show off a new dress. As she twirled, leapt and spun, the music faded back again, but the girl remained, giving Adren strength.

As the unicorn lifted its head, she rose to her feet. Lord Watorej and his officers had formed a semicircle around her and the unicorn, Nadin behind them. The light, filtered as it was through a lattice of cedar, came to rest on the forest floor as graceful as a deer. Beneath her feet, the moss- and needle-covered ground released the sharp scent of pine. A chipmunk chattered somewhere behind her, followed up by the cranky squawks of jays. Every scene, no matter how pastoral, had its own share of grumps.

"Lord Watorej, I lied." Adren could tell he wanted to do something about this, but he stopped when she held his gaze and didn't let go. "The unicorn can't help you. And the potion maker lied, too. She won't help you. She promised me a cure for madness at the cost of the money I stole from you and, when I brought it, at the cost of the sealskin. But she never gave it. And, with everything else she's done, I wouldn't trust her with anything more than a jail cell for the rest of her life. You want the curse broken? Accept the fact that you wanted to control a selkie more than you loved her, that it got you into this mess, and that I'm going to leave you to deal with it like the adult you are."

His face contorted under the power of the curse, and his hands trembled, causing the sword to wobble.

"If you leave now, I'll come after you!" he said.

"And I'll kill you. Remember the people I burned?"

The lord blanched.

Adren left.

When she and the unicorn returned to her camp, she started uncovering everything she'd hidden in order to put it into her pack, only to remember that she didn't have her pack. Lord Watorej must have taken it, along with the money and her knife.

After a steady stream of swearing, which alarmed the unicorn, she sat down. The unicorn went to her and prodded her with a hoof.

"And it was such a good exit, too!" she complained to it. Then she got up again and shook out the blanket.

Returning to town to… obtain a pack was out of the question with the lord's curse possibly still in effect. If she could wrap everything up in the blanket, maybe get creative with fitting things into her pockets, she might be able to make it to the next town and get a new pack without yelling at inanimate objects. Speaking of pockets, she still had on that awful livery, and had conveniently left a set of clothes at Nadin's house. This was why anyone with their head on straight would always bring another set while travelling. You never knew what might happen. She got out her spare clothing and changed, grumbling. The unicorn took the opportunity to wander off. Not out of her sight, but certainly out of her way.

In the beginning of her search for a cure for the unicorn, Adren had been so naive. She had known so little about humans and had thought all of them were decent, kind, and honest. For a while, this had served her well enough, and she had forgiven the few times that someone fell short of her expectations. The only problem was that she couldn't find a cure in the obvious places, which meant that she'd had to start looking under the veneer of morality that humans liked to keep their societies cloaked in. It had been more out of luck than skill that she had managed to escape every time she came across trouble but, as she got hurt, she had learned. And she had learned well.

It hadn't just been Pider. There had been others—so many others. In her dealings with them, she discovered people who had no qualms about lying, cheating, stealing, killing, if it meant monetary gain. They preyed on other humans, especially the gullible ones, and Adren had been so gullible. If she had not been able to turn invisible, if she had not known how to fight, she wouldn't have been able to avoid the worst that those people could have done.

For some time, she'd been willing to think that these traits only applied to the humans in that particular layer of society but, as she dealt with more people in more varied situations, she'd found echoes of those traits everywhere she went. Greed, pride, dishonesty, violence, a hunger for power, an indifference to others' need: all these and more she had seen and they disgusted her. Ordinary people, the ones that thought themselves at least moderately good, would sometimes talk about how morality got in the way of success and prosperity. They would brag about drunkenness and toying with the hearts of others. They would say one thing to a friend's face and another behind their back. They would break promises for the sake of convenience. And the most hateful thing of all was that they considered themselves pure while they condemned others for doing exactly what they did. People like that didn't deserve her gentleness, only her steel. That was how justice worked.

When she realized this and gave back what she had received, it had kept her safe from the corruption around her. Of course, they didn't like it. Those who had called her the White Changeling before because of the strangeness of her appearance began to use the name as a warning to those she might deal with. But no matter what humans called her or did to her, she would be able to fight back and she would be able to win. For herself, for the unicorn, for the lady and those in situations like hers. Her only regret in all of this was that she wasn't able to help Nadin. Even if he had to hide his magic from his own mother, he shouldn't have to bear the burden of her illness.

A good portion of her belongings fit in the blanket and the rest she'd managed to fit in her pockets, like she thought she would. Walking would be awkward, but the rope from her food cache would make sure that nothing would fall out while the bundle was attached to her back. So long as the unicorn didn't get ideas and try to pull a prank, that is. She hoisted it onto her back and checked to make sure the contraption was as solid as she thought. It was, so she removed it and sat back down.

If she had said what Lord Watorej needed to dislodge his pride, she shouldn't have to wait too long before Nadin came by to tell her that it had worked. She hadn't told him to do that, but it was fairly obvious that she would need the news. She hoped. The question, of course, was how long she could wait without endangerment if the curse still remained. Nadin had better be sensible enough to have figured that out for himself.

The unicorn spat a mouthful of fern onto Adren's lap, wrinkling its lips in distaste.

"What am I supposed to do with it?" she asked as she picked up the soggy vegetation.

If unicorns could shrug, it would have. Adren shook her head in mock dismay.

"Did I give permission to thee that thou mayest attempt imitation of Nadin's gestures?" She stuck out her tongue and threw away the greenery.

Ears pricked up, the unicorn lifted its head and Adren followed its gaze. Nadin waved as he approached. He had changed, too, and now sported a red cap on his head and a full pack on his back. Red. Of course it would be red. Under one arm, he carried something and, as he handed it to her, she breathed a sigh of relief. Her pack. She took it.

"Your knife's inside," he said. "Also hi."

Adren undid her bundle. "Why do you have one?"

"A knife?"

Unamused, Adren lifted her pack.

"Don't you want to hear what happened after you left?"

"Depends on how long it takes." She removed her belongings from the blanket, brushed the needles off, and then rolled it up.

"Well, Lord Watorej was angry after you left, and all the security officers were pretty confused." Nadin's words came out in a rush. "I don't blame them. I wouldn't know what to do if I

127

were them, either. He paced for a while, muttering. Then he stopped and stared for a long time. Then his hand went numb or something because he dropped his sword in this really weird way and yelled something that... uh... I don't want to repeat."

"So don't." The biggest items now packed, Adren emptied her pockets. Oh. Wait. The livery. That might have to go in last.

"And then it worked, Adren! I don't know how you did it, but it worked! The curse was gone."

"I figured that part out."

"Well, he told me to tell you thank you. Lady Watorej used to say things like you did to him a lot, and now he finally understands what she meant. Or is willing to. I'm not sure. He was really excited when he told me, and it was hard to understand everything he was saying. He'd been trying to love her all these years, even with the curse, and couldn't figure out why it wasn't working. I guess you were right—it wasn't love. I hope Lady Watorej will be able to forgive him someday. I don't think I've ever seen someone that happy."

"Good for him," Adren said. Why couldn't he have said, 'You broke the curse and Lord Watorej says thank you,' and left it at that? But this was Nadin, after all. She sighed. "Why didn't he come tell me in person?"

"He said he's too busy putting the potion maker in jail and finding a legal way not to let her out again, like you suggested."

"Really?" A one-sentence answer. It was a miracle.

"Really."

"So what about that pack?"

"I wanted to ask if I could come with you."

Adren stopped packing. Nadin looked at his feet and scratched his nose.

"What about taking care of your mother?"

"That's why I want to come. I've run out of options here, and I haven't found out what's wrong with her. You're looking for a cure for the unicorn, and I could never do this by myself, so I thought we might be able to help each other as we go. Lord Watorej promised to take care of my mother while I'm gone, to thank me for… whatever he thinks I did to help. And he gave me what I'd need to travel. Unless…" He gestured to the unicorn.

"It can't heal your mother. We tried."

"You went into my house and tried even though you hate humans?" Nadin's eyes shone with tears. Feeling uncomfortable, Adren nodded. "Thank you. Does that mean you'll let me come? I have everything with me, including food."

"Let me think." He nodded, so she finished packed. Slowly.

Nadin had been helpful, this she couldn't deny, and his skills would be useful to her in future. Perhaps he could teach her to use her magic, if she ever decided she needed that. Beyond that, he was loyal, almost to a fault.

On the other hand, his confidence issues could cause more trouble than his help was worth. His talkativeness would take a long time to get used to and, though she didn't know by how much, she was sure he'd slow her down while travelling. That, and despite all his words, he didn't always give her all the relevant information, like the lady's sleepwalking, and tended to give a lot more information she didn't need, like, well, just now. There was also his tendency to try to make a plan for everything. She shuddered. And was he only part human, like she hoped?

And yet, when he found out the lady was a selkie, he'd taken it upon himself at once to free her. It was as if he'd become immovable. In almost every other circumstance, he'd gone along with what Adren wanted, but the moment he found a captive magical creature, he would have done anything to see her out of her cage. That was something Adren couldn't ignore.

"Do you remember the footman who thought we were… together?" asked Nadin. Adren nodded, annoyed at the interruption of her thoughts, but not so much that she did anything more than fold the livery. "Lord Watorej said he had too many servants and that he needed to let some go, so I told him to fire the footman. I thought you'd want to know."

Oh, excellently done.

"You're not keeping the livery, are you?" he asked, eyeing it with concern. Adren grinned.

"Verily, I shall abscond with it." Nadin looked blank and she sighed. Evidently, he didn't understand the dialect. "I'm keeping it. Lord Watorej has my money."

"Except you stole—" He bit his lip. He was right, of course, but he seemed eager to please her so that she'd agree to his request. His attempt to make her think well of him reminded her of why he kept his magic hidden from those around him.

"Nadin, you know as well as I do what you told me about the Sight is nonsense. Where does your magic really come from?" She didn't think his explanation would differ from hers, but she wanted to hear it from his own lips.

He swallowed, then broke their gaze and rubbed his nose with his fist. "I can't tell you." His voice was raw with a mix of emotions she couldn't identify. Adren tried to meet his eyes, but he wouldn't let her. She thought of the dark place in her mind. The image of the dancing girl and the crying man, all that her magic could catch before they disappeared back into the blackness. While his mind worked so differently than hers, she understood just how many reasons someone might be unable to speak the truth, no matter how strong the confrontation.

The unicorn, bored with their conversation, butted Adren in the back with its nose. Its impatience and desire to leave rang clear within her, and her own emotions reflected the same back.

"You can come with me," Adren said, closing her pack. Nadin's whole face lit up.

"Really?"

"No, I was speaking hypothetically." She raised an eyebrow, shouldered the pack, and stood. "Are you ready?"

Nadin grinned and, when he came beside her, she turned and they started off, the unicorn following behind. Chickadees sang, their two-note call cheerful in spite of the overcast sky, and Adren let everything relax as she walked through the trees and breathed the fresh air.

Nadin could keep his secrets. At least he knew what his were.

About the Author

Thea van Diepen hails from the snowy land of Canada and that fairest of cities, Edmonton, Alberta. She is, of course, entirely unbiased, due to her Bachelor's in psychology (wait, that's not how that works...) and is obsessed with Orphan Black, Madeleine L'Engle's books, and nerdy language things.

When Thea was eight years old, she took a test in school that required her to write a story. This prospect excited her greatly, and she decided to write an epic fantasy adventure. Upon opening the test, she discovered she had to incorporate a girl going on a hike with her family. Thinking fast, she opened the story with said hike, dropped the girl through a hole into a magical world, thereby ditching the girl's family up on the mountainside, and happily wrote whatever she wanted until the end of the test.

Her website is expectedaberrations.com, home of all things that lie on the edge of the bell curve, and she can be contacted via that site in English or French. If you *do* email her in French, though, please don't ask her to count in it as she tends to skip numbers ending in six entirely by accident.

Acknowledgements

Thank you to:

Roberto Calas for designing an amazing cover (and for putting up with me).

EJ Clarke at Silver Jay Media for being an awesome editor willing to go the extra mile to hit a tight deadline and for adding a phrase to the story that made me stop and laugh for about a minute because it was just that perfect.

Margaux Yiu for giving a typography workshop years ago. I never would have been able to make these words look this pretty if not for you.

The writers in the Forward Motion chatrooms who helped me figure out ways to wake up a unicorn: Inkling, NPhoenix (even if you *were* in an odd mood that day), and Gerri.

Lewinna Solwing, for giving me feedback before I started editing and thereby helping me catch things that needed fixing early on. And for giving me plot bunnies every time I read your stories. Though distracting, it is still always delightful.

Lizzie Fowler, for giving feedback both before and after my edits, and for letting me read your stories-in-progress. One day, I will come and visit you in person, and it will be awesome.

Taryn Hunchak for always being willing to read and listen to all the things, even when I'm not even sure if all the things make sense. You're far more tolerant of spoilers than I, for which I am grateful. And also for all your superb help with editing. I don't know how I would have gotten it done without you. I think it goes without saying: you're a fantastic best friend.

And to God, for giving me the courage to write a whole freaking series, for encouraging me every step of the way, and for providing me with everything I need to thrive. Without you, I could never have written this book. Thank you.

Also by Thea van Diepen

Dreaming of Her and Other Stories
The Illuminated Heart (also available in paperback)

Go to Thea's author page on Amazon to find out more!

...and coming in 2016:

Like Mist Over the Eyes

Adren and Nadin meet a fairy who is quick to offer her people's
help in getting the cures they seek... but can she be trusted?

Made in the USA
Charleston, SC
11 October 2015